'I'm sure you'll soon have all the information you want.' He laid his hands on her shoulders, his grasp gentle, his fingers warm and strong, causing a ripple of heat to flow through her.

It was odd, but all at once as he held her she became strangely conscious of her femininity. It was confusing. She was so used to taking charge, to being in control, and yet with just one simple act he had made her overwhelmingly conscious of his powerful masculinity.

'Take time to ease yourself into the job,' he said. 'It will all work out—you'll see.' Then he smiled, his blue eyes homing in on her face, taking in the faint line that creased her brow and the look of uncertainty that hovered around her eyes and mouth. 'You'll be fine, Alex,' he murmured. 'It's good to have you here.'

Then he released her and strode briskly away, leaving Alex to stare after him in a bewildered fashion. Somehow she couldn't help thinking he was fobbing her off, albeit in a kind and gentle manner, and if he was an example of what she might expect from the staff here it was clear she was in for a tricky time from the outset. His easy charm had befuddled her senses and she was finding it hard to come to terms with that. It knocked her off track, and she wasn't used to that at all.

Dear Reader

It takes all sorts to make a world, doesn't it? Some people are driven to make a success of their careers to the point where they lose sight of what really matters. Others are serene and laid-back, taking life as it comes and never getting overly concerned about anything.

This set me to thinking. What if two such people met and struck sparks off one another? How could a relationship ever work between them—especially if neither of them was looking for anything permanent?

And that's exactly the problem that confounded Callum and Alex when they met and clashed in the A&E department.

Alex had so much to cope with after adversity had struck her family, so she wasn't in any mood to tread softly around anyone who didn't agree with her attempts to reorganise the department, despite the fact that she was trying to save it from closure.

Would Callum be the one to break the ice and show her what it was to be a warm, loving woman?

With best wishes

Joanna Neil

THE TAMING OF
DR ALEX DRAYCOTT

BY
JOANNA NEIL

First published in Great Britain 2011
by Mills & Boon, an imprint of Harlequin (UK) Limited.
Large Print edition 2011
Harlequin (UK) Limited, Eton House,
18-24 Paradise Road, Richmond, Surrey TW9 1SR

© Joanna Neil 2011

ISBN: 978 0 263 21772 8

Harlequin (UK) policy is to use papers that are natural, renewable and recyclable products and made from wood grown in sustainable forests. The logging and manufacturing process conform to the legal environmental regulations of the country of origin.

Printed and bound in Great Britain
by CPI Antony Rowe, Chippenham, Wiltshire

When **Joanna Neil** discovered Mills & Boon®, her lifelong addiction to reading crystallised into an exciting new career writing Medical™ Romance. Her characters are probably the outcome of her varied lifestyle, which includes working as a clerk, typist, nurse and infant teacher. She enjoys dressmaking and cooking at her Leicestershire home. Her family includes a husband, son and daughter, an exuberant yellow Labrador and two slightly crazed cockatiels. She currently works with a team of tutors at her local education centre, to provide creative writing workshops for people interested in exploring their own writing ambitions.

Recent titles by the same author:

BECOMING DR BELLINI'S BRIDE
PLAYBOY UNDER THE MISTLETOE
THE SECRET DOCTOR

CHAPTER ONE

'LOOK how many strawberries I picked,' seven-year-old Sarah announced, coming into the kitchen. She placed a wicker basket on the table, filled to the brim with fruit. 'There's loads,' she said, her blue eyes bright with excitement. 'Can we have some for breakfast?'

Alex looked at the lush fruit. 'Yes,' she murmured, 'of course…and as there's such a lot, perhaps we ought to take some round to Mrs Marchant next door? I've noticed she's usually up and about at this time of the morning.'

Sarah nodded. 'I'll go, if you like.' She smiled. 'I like Mrs Marchant. She's kind…but I think she must be quite old, you know, or poorly? She always looks a bit tired and sometimes she says she has to go and sit down for a while…but she's always nice. She gave me some toffees when I took the magazine round there yesterday.'

'I want to take the strawberries,' five-year-old James chimed in, his eyes lighting up at the mention of toffees. 'You went last time.' He glared at his sister and began to tug at the basket.

Sensing impending disaster, Alex intervened. 'We'll all go,' she said, taking hold of the basket and moving it from harm's way. 'Now, finish your breakfast, both of you. We don't have much time before we have to leave for school. And you need to go back upstairs to your bedroom and find your PE kit, James.'

'I don't like that bedroom,' James complained, scowling at Alex across the kitchen table, a lock of brown hair falling across his forehead. 'It's too small. Why can't I have the room with the window seat?'

'Because we talked about this…' Alex murmured. 'And you chose the one that looked out over the orchard.' She inspected the contents of his lunch box and then clipped the lid in place.

'So?' He hunched his shoulders. 'That doesn't matter, does it? I changed my mind. I can swap with Sarah.'

'No, you can't.' His sister batted that one away

before the idea could take root, her fair hair quivering with indignation. 'I want the one where I can see the garden… I chose it…and I picked the colours and Auntie Alex has already started painting the walls for me. So it's mine.'

'Perhaps we can rearrange the furniture in your room to make it better for you,' Alex said, glancing at James. She pushed his lunch box into his school bag and closed the zipper. 'I made you egg mayonnaise sandwiches, and there are cracker biscuits with ham and cheese. And don't forget to screw the lid tight on your drink bottle when you use it, or we'll have another mess in your bag like the one we had last week.'

'I don't like egg maynaze.' James's chin jutted and his grey eyes took on a mutinous glint.

Alex held back the sigh that had started to build up in her chest. She raised dark brows. 'You told me it was your favourite.'

He gave her a disdainful glance. 'That was yesterday. Today I like peanut butter.'

'Well, I'm sorry about that, James, but I really don't have time to start over.' Alex flicked back her long chestnut hair so that it settled in a gentle flurry across her shoulders, and handed him the bag. 'We have to get you and Sarah to school, and I have to go to work.' She checked her watch. 'Do you remember what I told you? This is my first day in the new job, and I need to be at the hospital on time.'

'Will you be in trouble if you're late?' Sarah's anxiety sounded in her voice. 'Mummy said she always got an ear bending from the boss if she wasn't at work for nine o'clock.' She frowned. 'I think that must hurt a lot. I wouldn't like it if it anyone pulled my ears.'

'How could that happen to Auntie Alex?' James said in a scornful tone. 'She's the boss. She can do what she likes.'

Alex smiled. 'Not exactly, James. There are several bosses in my department...but the fact is, if you're in charge you need to lead by example... show people the right way of doing things...so it's even more important that I get there on time.'

Sarah's face still bore a worried expression, so she added gently, 'Ear bending just means the boss would talk to your mother about where she was going wrong.'

'Really?' Sarah's blue eyes brightened. 'Well, I think he must be sorry, anyway, 'cos he sent Mummy some flowers. There was a card, and it said, *Get well soon.*'

She frowned again, and Alex gave her a hug. 'We all hope for that, Sarah. At least your mum and dad are in good hands. They're being looked after by the very best doctors.'

For once, James had nothing to say, and Alex sent him a quick, thoughtful glance. He seemed to be coping well enough in the aftermath of his parents' accident, but she suspected his new-found belligerence was all tied up with what had been going on in his life this last few weeks. She would have to keep a keen eye on both children for the foreseeable future.

A few minutes later they left the house and went next door. It was a minute or so before Jane Marchant answered Alex's knock, but when she did her smile was welcoming and she invited them inside.

'We can only stop for a minute or two,' Alex said, following her neighbour into the neat, pine kitchen. 'We just wanted to bring you these strawberries, and to make sure that you're all right.'

Jane stared at the fruit, her mouth dropping open in awe. 'Just look at that fruit—so ripe and juicy.' Her eyes glimmered with appreciation. 'I'll enjoy those with my tea—and I could make a lovely strawberry sponge cake. You'll have to come and share it with me.' She looked at the children, who nodded with enthusiasm at the suggestion. 'Thank you for this,' she said, embracing all three of them with her smile. 'It was very thoughtful of you.'

'Just don't go overdoing it,' Alex warned her. 'I know what you're like when you get started with the baking. I've been worried about you just lately, especially after that dizzy spell you had the other day. Are you still getting the headaches?'

Jane nodded. 'But you don't need to worry yourself over me, love. I'll be fine. Like I said, the doctor's been trying me with different tablets to see if we can calm things down. I probably just need to take things more slowly, that's all. I've perhaps done too much in the garden. I've been trying to tackle the weeds—you know yourself what a job that can be when you have an acre or so to look after.'

'I do.' Alex's lips made a downward curve. 'I'm still wondering what possessed me to take on that rundown house next door, with its dilapidated orchard and all those outbuildings.' Her mouth flattened. 'It just seemed like a good idea at the time.'

'I love it,' Sarah said. 'The garden's all wild and raggedy, and there's lots of fruit bushes all tangled up. And there's masses of strawberries...' she made a wide circle with her arms '...just spreading out all over the place.'

'It's like a jungle,' James put in, ignoring Alex's faintly amused groan. 'We can play explorers, hunting the bad people.' He began to make swashbuckling moves with an imaginary sword.

Sarah looked at Jane once more. 'I can help you with the garden,' she offered. 'Any time you like.'

'Thank you, sweetheart.' Jane beamed at the little girl. 'You're a treasure. Alex must be so happy to have you with her.'

'It's true,' Alex agreed. 'Both she and James

have been good as gold, helping with the move.' She frowned. 'But as far as your tablets are concerned, I'm not so sure that they're doing the job.' She glanced at Jane. Her neighbour was in her early sixties, a slender woman with brown, wavy hair and pale features. As Sarah had pointed out in her innocent way, she didn't look at all well. 'I really think you ought to go back to your doctor and ask him to do some tests to find out if there's a specific cause of the high blood pressure that might have been overlooked—especially since you're having other symptoms, like the back pain and the muscle spasms.'

Jane looked doubtful. 'I really don't like to bother the doctor any more. I've already been back several times and he's doing what he can to keep everything in check.'

'Even so,' Alex commented, 'as a doctor myself, I think your symptoms need to be looked into a bit more. I worry about leaving you on your own during the day while I'm at work. Is there no one in the family who can come and look out for you?'

Jane shook her head. 'There's only my nephew.

We're very close—in fact, he's more like a son to me. His parents, my brother and his wife, are out of the country, working on various projects.' Her features softened. 'He's such a lovely young man. I think the world of him…and he comes to visit whenever he's able. We often talk on the phone. I'm sure he'd do anything for me, but I know he's busy and I don't want to burden him with my problems.'

Alex's brows drew together. 'Maybe you should think twice about that—after all, he'd want to know if you were ill, wouldn't he?'

'Of course, but it won't come to that. I'll be fine. Besides, he has enough troubles of his own to deal with right now…' She pulled a face 'There's to be some kind of audit at work, apparently, and he has to figure out how to keep the chiefs off his back. He says they've appointed a new manager to whip the department into shape, and the last thing he needs is some busybody poking his nose into all the corners to see how they do things and then use it against him to turn all his carefully organised systems upside down.'

Alex's eyes widened a fraction, and she let out

a small breath. Managers were never popular. 'I see what you mean…he does seem to have a lot on his plate at the moment, doesn't he? But I think you're more important than any of that. I wonder if he could find time to help occasionally…with the garden, maybe?'

'Oh, he does what he can.'

James was beginning to show signs of restlessness, wandering about the room, peering at all the fine porcelain plates and glassware on display. He ran his fingers over the smooth lines of a ceramic cookie jar and then began to reach for a chicken-shaped timer, intent on examining its flamboyant red comb and wattles.

'I think it's time we made tracks,' Alex murmured, stopping to give Jane a quick hug. She'd only known this woman for a couple of weeks, but already it was as though they'd been friends for a lifetime.

'Let's go,' she said, handing Sarah her school bag. 'With any luck we'll get to school before the first whistle goes.'

Jane went with them into the hall. 'See you later,' she said.

'I don't like school,' James began as Alex shepherded them out through the front door. 'Mrs Coleman won't let me do painting. She made me sit in the reading corner instead. I don't like reading...'

He was still complaining as Alex bundled them into the car. 'It's a shame you're not happy, James, but it's nearly the end of term, you know, and you'll be able to look forward to the summer holidays.' She glanced at him. 'Fasten your seat belt. You know, if you want to paint, you have to remember to keep your brushes to yourself and resist the temptation to daub the other children. Mrs Coleman said she'd explained it to you. Perhaps you could tell her that you'll be sensible if she'll let you have another go.'

'Yes—well, I don't like her, either.' James clamped his lips together and squinted at the road ahead through narrowed eyes.

Alex checked that Sarah was safely installed in the back seat with a good space between her and her brother, and then drove towards the school. It was about a mile away from the house, along a winding country lane, and the drive was a pleasant one, though even that was not enough to calm her increasingly stretched nerves.

Had she taken on too much, making the decision to look after her brother's children? In itself, it shouldn't have been too difficult, but alongside the new job at Oakdale Hospital, and adding in the fact that she'd had to move to Somerset to be close to where they used to live, the stress was beginning to pile up. Her once calm and orderly life had been turned upside down. Everything was chaotic.

Not that there was much she could do about any of it. The car accident that had injured her brother and his wife had wreaked havoc with all their lives.

'Bye,' she said when they arrived at the school. 'Take care. Be good.' She kissed the children and hugged them and then watched for a minute or two as they met up with friends and went to stand in line for their teachers.

Then she headed back along the main road to town and her new place of work. The hospital was a few miles inland from the sea, and she drove towards it now, past the soft, rolling hills of the Quantocks, their slopes richly carpeted with heather and occasional dark oases of green woodland.

At the hospital, she parked in her designated place, and then made her way to the A and E department. She pulled in a deep breath, straightened her shoulders and walked into the main reception area. This was a new challenge, a difficult task that she'd been assigned, and she would need to have her wits about her. She was a little apprehensive about what lay in store, but she was determined to make the best effort she could.

Her first impression of the unit was a pleasant one. Everything seemed relatively calm in there. The treatment rooms were occupied, with patients being tended by medical staff, and the whiteboard showed the status of admissions and stage of treatment.

Across the room, a doctor was standing by the desk, chatting to nurses, until, after a moment or two, he noticed Alex and came over to her. He was good looking, long and lean, immaculately dressed in dark trousers and a white, self-striped shirt, finished off with a muted tie in a pale shade of blue.

'Hi, there,' he said. 'Can I help you? I guess you're not a patient, or you'd have been directed to the waiting room.' His voice was easy on the ear, deep and well modulated, and there was a warmth about him that made it seem as though he was genuinely interested in her. He had black hair, cut short to frame his angular features, and his eyes were a vivid blue, alert and enquiring.

'That's right. Yes, thank you, I'm looking for...' she checked his name badge '...Dr Brooksby.' She smiled. 'I believe I've found the very man I want.'

He laughed. 'Well, that's not something I get to hear every day...but more than welcome, all the same, coming from someone who looks as good as you.' His glance shimmered over her, taking in the tailored, dove-grey suit she was wearing, with the pencil-slim skirt and the jacket that nipped in at her slender waist. His gaze came to rest on the burnished, silky swathe of her hair, lingering there for a while longer than was absolutely necessary.

'Anything I can do for you, you only have to say.' His manner was open and friendly, his blue eyes quizzical, inviting her to offload any worries or problems she might have.

'That's very kind of you.' She let her glance roam fleetingly around the department. 'I must say, it's good to come to an A and E unit and find the atmosphere so relaxed and easygoing. That must be quite unusual, or perhaps I've come at a particularly quiet time? Either way, I imagine your bosses must be pleased with the way you run things around here.'

'You'd think so, but actually they're bringing in new management. And as to being quiet, it only appears that way—we've just finished dealing with the aftermath of a road accident, and now we're taking a breather and making the most of things...before the new manager comes along to sort us out and tell us where we've been going wrong.' His mouth made a rueful slant. 'Sorry to offload that way. It's a sore point. He's supposed to put in an appearance some time today so we're all on tenterhooks.'

A small ripple of dismay ran through her. This

was definitely not going to be an easy ride, judging by his comments. 'Oh, I see.' She reflected on what he'd said for a second or two, before venturing, 'Maybe he'll find that everything's perfectly in order?'

'What a refreshing idea.' He gave a wry smile. 'Unfortunately, I very much doubt it. He's a bean-counter, sent to trim us to the bone. This is the NHS, after all.' He pressed his well-shaped lips together briefly. 'Enough of my problems, though. What can I do for you, Miss…?'

'It's Dr,' she answered carefully. 'Dr Draycott. Alex.'

He stared at her, his mouth dropping open a little until he recovered himself. 'Alex Draycott?' he repeated, cautiously.

She nodded. 'That's right.' She studied him. 'You look as though you're taken aback by that. Is something wrong?'

Slowly, he shook his head. 'No, not at all. It's just that…well…you're a woman.'

She smiled. 'That's very observant of you.'

He was still staring, and she prompted gently, 'Is that likely to be a problem for you?'

'Uh… No, of course not. It's just that, well, Alex is a man's name, isn't it? We were expecting a man.' He frowned, looking at her in a slightly accusatory fashion. 'And I thought you were maybe a relative concerned about one of our patients.'

'I'm not.'

'No, I see that now.' His frown deepened. 'So you're the new doctor/manager who's come to join the unit?'

She hesitated. 'Um…bean-counter was how you put it, I think.' She gave him a wryly amused look, her grey eyes taking in his obvious unease. 'It's odd how defensive people become whenever managers arrive on the scene, isn't it? And it's totally unnecessary, you know—after all, we're all in this together, aren't we, working for the greater good of the hospital? I have a job to do, but it doesn't have to put us at odds with one another.'

'Doesn't it?' He appeared sceptical. 'Perhaps you aren't aware that your reputation has gone before you? We've all heard how you wielded the axe at your last hospital. There were job cuts and ward closures.'

She sent him a quick look, her grey eyes troubled. 'Sometimes, no matter how you try to preserve what's already in place, it becomes impossible in the end, if budget restrictions are too tight. But in all fairness to me, I did manage to keep the department open, I kept the job losses down to natural wastage, and I put new measures in place so that some patients could be tended to elsewhere.'

'You didn't stay around, though, did you, once your job was done?' His blue gaze was flint sharp. 'Was that because you found the atmosphere suddenly less friendly?'

The attack was swift and unexpected and Alex felt a knot tighten in her stomach. 'I left for personal reasons,' she said, a catch in her voice. 'It was nothing to do with the job. My circumstances changed, and my contract had come to an end anyway. I chose not to renew it.' Even the memory of that time, when she had first heard about her brother's accident, was enough to make the blood drain from her face.

He studied her thoughtfully, and perhaps he realised that he had touched a nerve, because he said softly, 'I'm sorry. That was uncalled-for on my part. Put it down to tension, if you will. We're all a little on edge here, uncertain about what the future holds for us and for the department. Of course, you were just doing your job.'

He laid a hand lightly on her elbow. 'Perhaps I should take you along to the doctors' lounge and offer you a cup of coffee? It was thoughtless of me not to suggest it before. It's just that your arrival threw me off balance for a minute or two. We weren't expecting you until later this morning.'

'No, I realise that…but I thought it would be as well to come in early and get the feel of the place.'

'I expect I would have done the same,' he said, leading the way along the corridor to the lounge. 'I think you'll like it here. Everyone's very friendly, and we work well together for the most part. The only real problem is the one that faces all hospital trusts. We're struggling with budget deficits and the department is under threat of being closed down. Dr Langton, the chief executive, has been warning us that it's a possibility.'

Alex frowned as they entered the room. 'I was appointed by the board to try to make sure that doesn't happen.'

His mouth made a wry twist. 'Well, let's hope you can work wonders. It's a difficult job you've taken on, and in some ways management can turn out to be a poisoned chalice. Not many would want to do it.'

'I suppose not.' She was thoughtful for a moment or two. 'But in all the years I've worked as a doctor, I've come across things that aren't working as well as they should, and over time I began to think that perhaps if I went into management, I might be able to make a difference.'

'You've obviously put a lot of thought into it. For myself, I prefer hands-on medicine one hundred per cent of the time.'

'And I'm sure that must be the reason you've done so well for yourself. I've heard nothing but good things about you, from the occasional article in the press and the medical journals, as well as from Dr Langton. You've been at Oakdale for some time, haven't you?'

'Yes, for several years. I came here originally as a registrar and then I was offered the post of consultant. I love it here…it's like a home from home for me.' He grinned. 'Mind you, I think medicine's in my blood. It's been there ever since I was a child, pretending to be an army surgeon to my wounded toy soldiers.'

She laughed softly, trying to imagine him as a youngster. 'I can see you in my mind's eye,' she said, 'bandaging your action figures. Though I expect most boys wouldn't bother too much with those who'd been invalided out.' Still, even James had made a crutch for a toy soldier that had lost its plastic leg, painstakingly taping the wooden stick to its hand.

He made a wry smile. 'Maybe not.' He went over to the coffee machine to one side of the room and poured hot liquid into two mugs. 'Do you take milk and sugar?' he asked, and she nodded.

'Both, thanks.' She sniffed the air appreciatively. 'That smells good.'

He nodded. 'It's one thing I look forward to around here. Decent coffee.' He waved her to a chair. 'Have a seat and make yourself comfortable.' He came to sit close to her and swallowed his coffee, savouring the taste and taking a moment to relax. 'So, tell me about yourself,' he said quietly, his glance moving over her and coming to rest briefly on the smooth shapeliness of her long legs. 'From what I heard, you've moved here from Herefordshire? I suppose that means this job must have had some special appeal for you?'

'I thought it would give me the best of both worlds, the chance to work in paediatric emergency, which is what I like doing best—it's what I specialised in—and at the same time it allows me to take on a managerial role.' She clasped her cup in both hands, feeling the comforting warmth spread slowly through her. 'But the main reason I'm here is because I have family who have settled in Somerset.'

'Your parents?'

She shook her head. 'My brother and his family. My parents do have a home here, but they're away at the moment, because of my father's job. He's a troubleshooter for an oil company, so he tends to travel a lot.'

He gave a brief smile. 'That's something we have in common, then. My parents have always travelled far and wide, as far back as I can remember.' A fleeting sadness came into his eyes and she studied him thoughtfully for a moment or two. Had that been a problem for him?

'Perhaps I've been lucky,' she murmured. 'My parents were always there for me while I was growing up. It was only when I started work as a doctor that they began to travel further afield.' She would have liked to ask him about his family, but something warned her that this might be the wrong time to do that. She didn't want to blunder into areas that might cause problems, especially on her first day. Perhaps when she knew him a little better…

'It must have been difficult for you, uprooting yourself,' he said. 'Did you manage to find a place of your own, or are you renting while you look around?'

'I thought about renting. Back in Herefordshire

I'd taken out a lease on a flat, but it ran out—another reason why it seemed feasible to make the move to Somerset. I planned to do the same down here, but then I saw this big, old house on the market, going for a song, and I decided to snap it up. It was purely an impulsive action—not like me at all, but something about it appealed to me. Of course, the reason it was going so cheap is because it needs a lot of work…' She pulled a face. 'And the owner wanted a quick sale.'

'But things are working out fairly well for you, overall?'

She nodded. 'I think so. I hope so.' She drank her coffee and looked around. 'As I see it right now, though, my biggest challenge is going to be this job. According to Dr Langton, the hospital is deep in debt and the accident and emergency department is at risk. I want to do all I can to keep it safe, but it means taking some measures that might not be all that popular.'

She braced herself. 'In fact, I think I ought to make a start on getting to grips with the job right now—it's been good to spend a few minutes in here, and I appreciate you taking a break and having coffee with me, but perhaps now I should start to familiarise myself with the way things work around here.' She glanced at him. 'Mr Langton suggested you might be available this morning to give me an insight into the way you run things—where and when you use agency staff, for instance—and perhaps you could let me see your drugs list, so I can gain some idea of expenditure in that area?'

He frowned. 'Are you sure you want to do that on your first day? Wouldn't you prefer to take a general look around and get to know some of the staff? I'm sure they're all anxious to meet their new colleague.'

She nodded. 'Of course, and I want to meet them, but I don't want to intrude on them while they're busy. I'll definitely make time to introduce myself to them through the course of the day. For the moment, though, I think it would be better if I were to spend time with you...going through the workings of the department.'

'Hmm...yes...' He seemed to be distracted all at once, and glanced at the watch on his wrist.

'Unfortunately, I have an emergency to attend,' he said, getting to his feet. 'So I'm afraid you'll have to forgive me. Maybe we could get together some other time?'

She frowned. 'But I understood that you would be free from clinical duties this morning for a couple of hours. Is that not so?'

He nodded. 'But then this emergency came up…a thoracic injury, flail chest. He should be coming back from Radiology any time now.'

Alex stood up. 'But I was really hoping to make a start…'

'Of course. I appreciate that, but, you know, I don't actually have the figures you want right at this moment…you've caught me on the hop a bit there, and I really do have to go and check on my patient.' He gave her an encouraging smile. 'Perhaps it would be best if you go and find our registrar. He'll help guide you around the department. Ask him anything you want to know. He'll be only too happy to help you.'

'But I…' Alex gazed at him in confusion.

'I'm sure you'll soon have all the information

you want.' He laid his hands on her shoulders, his grasp gentle, his fingers warm and strong, causing a ripple of heat to flow through her. It was odd, but all at once, as he held her, she became strangely conscious of her femininity. It was confusing. She was so used to taking charge, of being in control, and yet with just one simple act he had made her overwhelmingly conscious of his powerful masculinity.

'Take time to ease yourself into the job,' he said. 'It will all work out, you'll see.' Then he smiled, his blue eyes homing in on her face, taking in the faint line that creased her brow and the look of uncertainty that hovered around her eyes and mouth. 'You'll be fine, Alex,' he murmured. 'It's good to have you here.'

Then he released her and strode briskly away, leaving Alex to stare after him in a bewildered fashion. Somehow, she couldn't help thinking he was fobbing her off, albeit in a kind and gentle manner, and if he was an example of what she might expect from the staff here, it was clear she was in for a tricky time from the outset. His easy charm had befuddled her senses and she was finding it hard to come to terms with that. It knocked her off track, and she wasn't used to that at all.

CHAPTER TWO

'IT CAN never be easy, can it, seeing your loved ones this way…even if you're a doctor?' The nurse was sympathetic, sensing Alex's distress. 'All I can say is that your brother's condition is stable at the moment. I hope that might be some comfort to you.'

'It is. Thank you.' Alex dragged her gaze away from the hospital bed. It was heart-rending to see her younger brother lying there, looking so fragile. He was deathly pale, his hair dark against his pillow, various tubes and drains coming from his body, and there were cables linking him to monitors. Ross, who had always been so vigorous and who could be relied on to brighten any room with his presence, was just a shadow of his former self.

'It was a nasty accident,' the nurse added, 'and there was a considerable amount of lung damage because of the broken ribs he suffered. That's why he's still on the ventilator, but he's receiving pain medication, so at least he should be fairly comfortable.'

Alex nodded. 'I know you're all doing everything you can for him.'

The nurse made a note of Ross's heart rate and blood-oxygen levels. 'Have you been to see his wife? I know she was badly injured, too.'

'Yes, I make a point of looking in on her every day. The doctors are treating her for a laceration to her liver, but they found there was some damage to her kidney as well. She's been through surgery, and she's in much the same situation as Ross, reliant on tubes and drips and monitors. Even so, she's fretting over the children.'

'I'm sorry.' The nurse laid a hand on Alex's arm. 'It must be very worrying for you, especially with the youngsters to consider. I think it's good that you've been bringing them in to see their parents, though.'

Alex sucked in a deep breath. 'Better for them to see what's happening, I thought. Otherwise their imaginations might cause them to worry even more. Their grandparents will be coming over at the weekend, so that should help to cheer them up a little.' Her mouth flattened. 'My parents have found it hard, being so far away when it happened. But they've worked out a schedule so that one or other of them will be over here to spend time with Ross for a good part of the week.'

'You said they were working abroad, is that right?'

Alex nodded. 'My father works for an oil company. It's a really difficult time for him right now, but all he can think about is Ross.'

'That's understandable.'

Alex spent a few more minutes by her brother's bedside until she finally had to acknowledge that time was getting on. She had taken a late lunch, but now she needed to go back to work. Reluctantly, she made her way to the ground floor of the hospital, heading for A and E.

Things were no easier in that department, either. Her work colleagues were uneasy, doubtful about her intentions in her role as manager, and worried regarding their job security.

Alex tried not to let it unsettle her. She would try to put their minds at ease, and she would do the best she could for the department. After all, she was her father's daughter, wasn't she, strong, determined, willing to put in every effort for a cause she felt to be worthwhile? And in these difficult times keeping the A and E department viable and open for business was surely the best outcome for everyone?

Today, though, she was here in her role as doctor, and now she glanced at the whiteboard as she walked over to the main desk. 'Katie, I'll take the three-year-old with fever in treatment room two.'

'Okay.' The triage nurse handed her the child's admission notes.

Alex headed for the treatment room. As she had told Callum, landing this job had given her the best of both worlds—management took up fifty per cent of her time, and working as a consultant emergency paediatrician took up the rest.

She glanced at the triage nurse once more as she passed by the desk. 'Is Dr Brooksby about?' She'd been on the lookout for him all morning.

Katie hesitated, tucking a strand of glossy black hair behind one ear. 'Um…last I saw of him he was in Resus.'

'Hmm.' Alex had already checked, and he certainly wasn't there now. 'Thanks, Katie. I'm sure I'll manage to hunt him out.'

She found him a minute or two later in the treatment room next to hers. He was checking an ECG printout, while at the same time assuring his patient that he was in safe hands.

'You've had a minor heart attack,' he told the middle-aged man lying on the bed, 'but we have things under control now. The medication should help to open up your blood vessels, and things should soon start to feel a lot easier. Just keep pulling on the oxygen.'

He glanced across the room as Alex put her head round the door. 'So there you are,' she said. 'I'm glad I've run into you at last. I've been searching everywhere for you.'

'What it is to be popular,' he murmured, winking at his patient. He adjusted the settings on the medication pump and checked the drip. 'What could be better than having a gorgeous young woman seeking you out?'

Alex pulled a face. He obviously knew how to charm the birds out of the trees. 'I know you've a lot on,' she murmured, 'but I really need you to go over the drug expenditure figures with me some time soon—and I noticed your casualty cards aren't up to date. We need to get them filled in so that we can check waiting times.'

'Yes, of course.' He nodded agreeably. 'I've been working on it. We always try to fill these things in on time, you know, but it can get pretty frantic around here, and it isn't always easy to keep up with the admin paperwork.' He sent her an engaging smile, inviting her to agree with him, his blue gaze shimmering over her so that she found herself unwillingly caught up in his masculine magnetism and his easygoing manner.

'Yes, well…um…' She blinked. It was thoroughly disconcerting, the way he managed to tip her off balance. What was she thinking? She made an effort to pull herself together. 'Maybe we could get together for a few minutes as soon as you've finished here and go through a few of the items we need to get to grips with? I'll be next door in the paediatric bay, working with a patient.'

'Sounds like a good idea. I'll see what I can do.' He was totally relaxed, completely unfazed by her request.

'Good. That's encouraging.' She slanted him a brief, searching glance. 'See you in a few minutes, then,' she murmured.

She left the room, with a friendly nod to the patient, who was looking much better than he had done a short time ago, and went to see the toddler next door.

The infant was lying on a trolley bed, clearly feeling too wretched and uncomfortable to be held in his mother's arms. A nurse was cooling him by holding a damp cloth to his forehead, but as Alex entered, she went to step aside.

'That's all right, Charlotte,' Alex said. 'You go on with what you're doing. I'm sure he'll feel much better for it.'

Alex smiled at the boy's mother. 'Mrs Stanhope, I understand Tom has been poorly for several days?'

The woman nodded. 'It's horrible to see him like this. He won't eat, he keeps being sick, and now he has a temperature. I'm really worried about him.'

'Of course you are.' She looked at Tom. 'The poor little chap looks really miserable.' She spoke gently to the boy. 'I'm going to try to make you feel a bit more comfortable, Tom,' she murmured, 'but I need to listen to your chest first…and maybe look at your tummy. Is that all right?'

The toddler looked uncertain, his lower lip trembling, and the nurse attempted to distract him by producing a teddy bear from a basket at the side of the bed. 'Look,' she said, 'Teddy's feeling poorly, too. His tummy hurts.'

Tom's eyes widened and he gazed at the toy, putting out a hand to feel his silky fur. Alex sent the nurse a grateful glance and gently began her examination. When she had finished, she said softly, 'That's all done now, Tom. You were very brave.'

The boy clutched the teddy to him. 'Teddy hurting,' he said. 'He feels sick.' Suddenly all the colour left his face and the nurse promptly moved forward with a kidney dish, holding it in place as he began to retch.

Alex went to sit next to the child's mother. 'We tested Tom's urine earlier,' she told her, 'and it looks as though he has a urinary infection of some kind. It's quite possible that his kidneys are inflamed, so I'm going to start him on a course of antibiotics. I'll give him the first dose by injection so that it will start to act quicker, but the rest we'll give by mouth.' She glanced at Charlotte and gave instructions about the medications. 'And that includes something to ease the pain and bring down his temperature.'

'Thank you.' Mrs Stanhope seemed anxious. 'How long will it be before he's better?'

'It could be two or three weeks… I feel we should admit him to hospital so that we can keep an eye on him—I know that's probably worrying for you, but we have to make sure we deal with this properly, right from the start, and of course that way he'll be on hand when we get the results of his urine culture back from the lab.'

Mrs Stanhope nodded. 'It's all right. I just want what's best for him.'

'That's good. I'll make the arrangements.' Alex stood up and went back to her small patient. 'Just a tiny jab,' she told him, preparing the antibiotic injection. 'It will all be over in a second or two.'

A few minutes later, she left the infant and his mother in Charlotte's capable hands, and went to look for Callum. He was nowhere to be found, not in any of the treatment rooms, or in Resus, or even out by the ambulance bay. She checked the quadrangle where staff sometimes took a breath of fresh air between seeing patients, but he wasn't there either.

She frowned. 'Any sign of Dr Brooksby?' she asked Katie as the nurse walked towards the reception area.

'None at all.' Katie shrugged lightly. 'I expect he's gone back to Resus.'

Alex suppressed a sigh. 'Not to worry,' she said. 'I dare say I'll catch up with him sooner or later.'

Katie nodded. 'That's how it is down here, unfortunately. Everyone's so busy.'

Alex's mouth made a flat line. Busy or not, they all had to work together to help streamline the department, or before too long the trust board would be calling for closures. One way or another they had to find time to co-operate with her. 'If anyone needs me, I'm heading over to Pathology,' she said.

She would take Tom's sample over to the lab herself for culture, and ask if the results could be hurried up. Once they knew the bacterial culprit, they could choose the most appropriate treatment for the child. The wide-spectrum antibiotic she had used was a catch-all for the most likely bacteria, but given the severity of the infection it was possible that they needed to use something more specific to counteract it.

She walked into the lab a few minutes later, shooting a quick glance around the room. Over to one side, by the workbenches, she saw a by-now familiar figure huddled over a rack of test tubes.

'So here you are,' she murmured, after handing over the specimen to the lab technician. 'I never would have thought to find you here, Dr Brooksby.'

He straightened, turning to look at her. 'I'm checking on some samples I sent for testing. I want to see how things are coming along, you know.'

'Really?' She inspected the label of the sample he was studying. 'Since when were you working with the staff on the geriatric ward? Was your patient sent there from A and E?'

He frowned. 'It's the wrong sample,' he said. 'My patient's elderly, but not geriatric.'

She sent him a cautious look, her grey eyes doubtful. 'You wouldn't be deliberately trying to avoid me, would you, Dr Brooksby?'

'Callum, please. Now, why on earth would I want to do that?'

'That's what I'm wondering. Only I was under the impression we were going to meet up in the treatment room a while ago. Didn't you agree to that?'

'Of course—though I believe what I actually said was that it was a good idea, which is not necessarily the same thing as saying I'd be there.

You can't guarantee anything in the hectic atmosphere of the A and E department.' He searched among the papers in a wire tray and grasped one in triumph. 'Found it,' he said. He held it up to her. 'My patient's results.'

She stared at him in frustration. 'Why is it that I have the feeling you're playing games with me?' she asked. 'You haven't actually completed the drug lists, have you? Or tried to catch up on filling in the waiting times on your casualty cards?'

He leaned back against the workbench, his long legs crossed at the ankles. 'Actually…uh… no, you're right. I haven't.' His mouth made a rueful shape. 'As I said before, I'm much more of a hands-on medic than someone who concentrates on keeping his paperwork up to date.'

His gaze ran over her, appreciation lighting his eyes as he took in the shapeliness of her figure outlined by her classically styled dress. 'I know you want to get on with updating your numbers and counting the financial cost of everything, but is it so essential that it's done right this minute? You've only been here a short time. Surely you need to take some time to settle in? And how about giving everyone a bit of leeway? Give them a chance to get used to the idea of you being around. That way people would be so much more on your side.'

She sighed. 'That would be so satisfying, wouldn't it…just to let everything hang easy for a while, gain a little popularity and then sit back and enjoy the ride?' There was amusement in her tone. 'I hardly think that's going to happen.' Her grey glance meshed with his.

'You don't?' He frowned.

'I don't. Why do you imagine I was brought in here? The executives were hardly going to appoint a pussycat to monitor things, were they?' She didn't wait for an answer. 'The hospital budget is badly overdrawn and the trust has to make drastic cuts if the services the public want and expect are to survive.' She drew in a deep breath. 'So that's where I come in. I have the task of auditing the department to find out where savings can be made…and if I don't come up with the right answers, the whole emergency unit is at risk—so it's not just my job on the line, but those of everyone who works here.' She studied him. 'You do understand that, don't you?'

He lifted his shoulders. 'Of course I do…it's just that I don't see why you can't hold fire for a while. The trust has been overspending for years—a few weeks isn't going to make much difference to the grand scheme of things, is it?'

She shook her head, causing her chestnut curls to swirl and shimmer under the overhead lights. 'That's where you're wrong, I'm afraid. I have to report back to the board at the end of each month. They aren't going to look kindly on me or the department if I show them an empty file.'

He watched the cloud of burnished hair drift and settle. 'You realise, don't you,' he countered, 'that the board will do what it wants, no matter what facts and figures you manage to produce? If they're set on closing the department, then ultimately that's what they'll do. They just need you to give them the firepower.'

She regarded him steadily. 'Well, I don't think that way about it at all. I believe that I can make a difference. I believe we can make savings in lots of ways. In fact, going on my experience with a young patient this morning, I've decided I want to start a separate audit into the treatment of children with urinary infections…let's see if we can't cut down on the number of ultrasound scans, and choose our drugs more wisely, so that we're not prescribing expensive ones where generic drugs will do better.'

She warmed to her theme. 'It's just a question of devising the forms for people to fill in whenever they treat a child—and at the end we'll collate all the information and see what savings we can come up with.'

He looked at her, aghast. 'Good grief, woman… don't you have enough to do without getting started on audits that aren't even part of your remit?'

'But it all comes down to the same thing in the end, don't you see? Savings are at the heart of everything.'

He relaxed, beginning to smile at her. 'I can see why you got the job…and I have to admire your persistence. You're so full of energy and enthusiasm—but there's more to life than work, you know. Where do you find time in all that for a social life—that thing called 'fun'—boyfriends, and so on?'

His glance drifted over her. 'You're a very attractive woman, and I'd have thought men would be queuing up to ask you out. Yet from what I've heard you don't have a significant other, you don't join the staff at the local pub—or even share lunch breaks with them. Isn't there something missing from your life?' His gaze became thoughtful. 'Or perhaps you've been hurt...' he said softly. 'Maybe someone let you down?'

She stared at him blankly for a moment or two. So he thought she was attractive? He'd said it before, but even so, it gave her a warm, fuzzy feeling, hearing him say it again. But as to the rest, when did she have time to socialise? Any spare time she had at work was spent on visiting her brother and his wife, and after work she needed to take care of the children.

'I see the hospital grapevine has been busy,' she murmured. 'Is nobody's life private around here?' She frowned. 'Though I could say the same for you. Snatches of gossip I've heard tell me you don't ever settle to a relationship—fear of commitment is how they put it, I think.'

He laughed. 'I don't see fear coming into it. Life's too short, and I'm having a good time just as I am—being footloose and fancy-free. Why would I want to change things?'

'Why indeed?' She smiled wryly. 'And much the same goes for me. I'm far too busy to even contemplate getting involved with anyone right now. Let the gossipmongers make of it what they will.'

'And they will, believe me.' He studied her. 'Why don't we fox them all and make a date for dinner—this evening, maybe? You should take time out, let yourself unwind a little.'

Unwind, with him? The thought had a dizzying effect on her. 'Thanks, but I really can't do that right now.' All the same, she conjured up a vision of the two of them together, taking a walk in the moonlight after a romantic meal at a restaurant, and all at once heat began to pool in her abdomen.

She couldn't let the idea take hold. It was impossible. She wasn't about to get involved with anyone, especially him, a man who seemed so laid back he made it seem as though she was positively racing through life in contrast. Anyway, she had far too much on her plate. The children relied on her to be there for them, her family life was chaotic, and, besides, he was simply trying to divert her, possibly even disarm her into the bargain, wasn't he?

His gaze flicked over her. 'That's a shame. Maybe some other time, then? I'm sure you'll feel all the better for a little rest and relaxation.'

She had the idea this was something he wouldn't give up on easily. 'I'll feel a whole lot better when I have your drug expenditure forms laid out on my desk,' she retorted swiftly. 'Along with a list of agency staff employed by the department over the last three months.'

She ignored his muffled groan as she made her way to the door. 'Any time in the next twenty-four hours will be fine.'

She was still debating how best to deal with Callum Brooksby when she made her way home later that day at the end of her shift. He was a thorn in her side, a devious, happy-go-lucky, aggravating man who gave the impression of being as difficult to catch as thistledown. Every time she had him within her sights, he somehow managed to whisk himself away, out of reach.

'Look what we've found,' Sarah said excitedly, greeting Alex as she went to collect the children from her neighbour's house later that day. Sarah led the way into the kitchen. 'Auntie Jane showed us how to collect honey from the beehives in the orchard. We've been putting it into jars. It smells of flowers.'

Alex sniffed at the glass pot Sarah thrust under her nose. 'So it does,' she said. 'I expect the bees have been visiting the apple blossom and the bramble bushes. That should make for good fruit later on in the season.'

She looked at Jane, who was standing by the fridge, looking pale and tired. 'You've been busy. Are you sure you should be taking on all this work? I feel bad enough that I'm asking you to watch the children for me.'

'Oh, I like having them around. Anyway, I volunteered to have them after school, and it's no trouble to collect a bit of honey.' Jane smiled. 'I expect you had no idea what a wealth of treasures you were gaining when you bought the property next door. Of course, I didn't let the children go near the hives when I collected the honeycombs, but they loved seeing the end result. They were fascinated.'

'It tastes funny,' James said, screwing up his nose. 'Yuk.'

'I like it,' Sarah said happily. 'We had some on pancakes and they were scrumptious.'

'It sounds as though you had a lot of fun.' Alex watched the children as they carefully spooned the golden honey into scrupulously clean jars. Jane sat down by the table and let them get on with it for a while.

'How have you been feeling, Jane?' Alex asked, giving her a long, thoughtful look. 'Have you been back to see your doctor?'

'Not yet.' Jane shook her head, and at Alex's small murmur of protestation she added, 'I know...I keep putting it off, and I shouldn't, but what's he going to do for me but give me more tablets? Nothing's working, so I might as well put up with things as they are.' As she spoke, she absently rubbed her back. 'The only that really gets to me is this pain, but I suppose I can take painkillers for that.' She sighed. 'But I guess that's old age creeping up on me.'

'I don't think so, Jane. I think it's something that needs to be investigated.'

She might have said more, but there was a brief tap on the kitchen door just then, and a moment later it opened, as a visitor stepped into the kitchen.

Alex pulled in a sharp breath.

'Hi, Aunt Jane,' Callum Brooksby said, going over to Jane and giving her a hug. 'How's my favourite aunt?'

'Oh, it's so good to see you,' Jane said, smiling. She looked at him with genuine affection. 'I was hoping you'd come round.'

He nodded. 'I know I've left it a little bit longer than usual. It's been a busy time lately, what with work and overseeing the builders at home.' Then he straightened and looked around, interested in seeing who had come to take tea with her.

His gaze met Alex's and they both stared at one another in shock.

'Alex?'

'Callum?' She blinked.

Callum frowned, his dark brows drawing together in a straight line. 'What on earth are you doing here?'

'I...I bought the house next door,' she said, stumbling a little over the words, still in shock. 'That's how I came to know your aunt—she's been good to me, looking after the children while I'm at work.'

'Children?' His expression became incredulous as he turned his attention to James and Sarah, happily spilling honey over the scrubbed pine table and the assembled jars. 'Good grief.' He looked back at Alex. 'I don't know you at all, do I?'

Jane looked from one to the other, a puzzled expression on her face. 'So you two have met before this?' She frowned. 'Of course, it must be the hospital—it didn't occur to me. I knew you were in Paediatrics, Alex, and, Callum, you're in

Emergency, but of course you must meet up on occasion.'

'All the while, Aunt Jane,' Callum agreed, a look of wonder coming over his face. 'We work in the same department.'

Alex was still trying to get over the shock. She studied him carefully. 'So you're the nephew?'

His head went back. 'Nephew? Why, who's been talking about me?' He looked at Jane, a glimmer of amusement coming into his eyes. 'It has to be you, doesn't it? You've only told her good things, I hope?'

'As if I'd do anything else,' Jane answered cheerfully.

Callum put an arm around her in a gesture of affection. 'She practically brought me up,' he told Alex. 'She's been like a mother to me.'

Jane patted his hand.

'Auntie Jane, can we go and play in the garden?' James asked, coming over to her and beginning to tug on her skirt.

'Yes, of course.' Jane's glance ran over him, and a line indented her brow. 'Perhaps we'd better get you cleaned up a bit first, though.'

James looked down at the honey trails that streaked his T-shirt. 'It's all right,' he said. 'I can do that.' He pulled his shirt up to his mouth and began to lick the sticky patches.

Sarah pulled a face. 'You are so gross,' she said in disgust.

'Why?' James responded, astonished. 'Am not.'

Callum began to laugh. 'Was I ever like that?' he asked his aunt, and she nodded. 'All the time.' She turned her attention back to the boy. 'I'll get a cloth.'

'No, don't do that. I'll see to everything,' Alex said, intervening when Jane would have stood up. 'You stay there and rest. You've done enough for one day.' She helped the children to wash their hands, before sending them outside, and then she began to clear up the mess on the kitchen table.

Jane tried to lend a hand, gathering up spoons and honeycombs, but Alex gently took them from her. 'You're already hurting,' she remonstrated softly. 'Let me do it.'

Callum frowned, looking at his aunt. 'What's this about you hurting? Is it your back again?'

Jane nodded. 'It's nothing for you to worry about,' she said. 'I'll be fine.'

'Hmm. Why don't you go and sit down in the living room, and I'll bring you a cup of tea? I'm sure you'll be much more comfortable in there.'

His aunt smiled. 'You're probably right. What a good idea.' She looked from one to the other. 'Anyway, I expect you young things have plenty to say to one another.'

She left the room, and a moment later, still frowning, Callum began to help with the clearing up. He placed sticky jars on the drainer, and flicked the switch on the kettle.

'I still can't get over seeing you here,' he said, looking at Alex. 'It's a small world, isn't it?'

'It certainly seems that way.'

He began to prepare a tray, setting out a cup and saucer, along with a plate of home-made biscuits. He smiled as he peered into the cookie jar. 'She's always loved baking,' he said, helping himself to an oat biscuit. He offered the jar to Alex. 'She let me help her when I was a child, but I'm not sure my efforts were all that brilliant. They tended to be misshapen, and a bit cracked around the edges.'

'Much like mine, then,' Alex said, helping herself to a biscuit, and they both chuckled. She looked at him, trying to imagine him as a child, mixing cookie dough or playing outside in the long garden. 'You said she was like a mother to you...does that mean you lived here with her?'

He nodded. 'For a good deal of the time, anyway.' He looked around. 'I love this house. It feels like home to me. In fact, I love the whole area.'

'And your parents? Where were they?'

'Mostly abroad, either in Africa or South America. I didn't see a lot of them in my teen years because they were off working on projects to improve the health of the underprivileged children out there. Things are much the same nowadays.'

'That must have been difficult for you.' Her grey eyes were sympathetic. She remembered how sad he'd been when he'd first mentioned his parents. 'You must have missed them.'

'I suppose so.' He frowned. 'But my aunt and uncle made up for it. They gave me a decent home life and showed me what it was like to be part of a loving family. Until then, nothing had ever been stable. My parents were always busy, working all hours, and we moved around constantly. There was no chance of putting down any roots.'

Alex was sad for him. He'd obviously not known what a loving family was like in his earlier years.

'You were lucky, then, that your aunt was able to take you in.'

'Yes, I was.' He poured tea into the cup. 'I'd better go and check on her, and take her the tea.'

Alex glanced at him and hesitated a second or two before saying, 'You know she's having problems with her blood pressure, don't you?'

He nodded. 'It was diagnosed some time ago. She's been prescribed a number of different medications over the past year or so.'

'Yes, that's what she said. But it seems to me that whatever her GP's giving her isn't working, and I suspect that's because he hasn't yet found the root cause of her problem. I'm wondering if she ought to have some tests done at the hospital.

She's suffering from a number of symptoms that need to be investigated...headaches, dizziness, pain in her back.'

A line etched itself into his brow. 'Her doctor's been taking care of her for years, though. She trusts him, and it's no easy thing to get her to go along to see anyone else.'

Alex's mouth flattened. 'Even so...I don't see how she can go on this way. She doesn't look at all well. Something needs to be done. In fact, I feel really guilty that I took her up on her offer to look after the children. It worries me that I'm putting too much on her.' She pulled in a deep breath. 'And I don't believe she's coping too well with the house and garden either. The weeds are beginning to overtake the borders, and it's all much more than she can manage.'

Callum gave Alex a perplexed stare. 'I mended the fence and tidied up the rockery a couple of weeks ago.'

Alex finished wiping the table with a flourish. 'I'm sure the stress of keeping up with the maintenance is taking a toll of her. Is there any chance you could arrange a more regular schedule? Find a local gardener who will come along and tidy things up, perhaps?'

He didn't say a word for a moment or two, but simply studied her as though he was deep in thought.

'You're very good at this sort of thing, aren't you?' he said at last, a note of wonder in his voice.

'This sort of thing?' She frowned. 'I'm afraid I'm not following you.'

'Organising people…deciding what needs to be done. I get the strongest feeling that not only am I being audited at work, but now you're taking stock of how I conduct my personal life as well.' He turned his blue gaze on her. 'I'm obviously done for. Maybe I should give in, here and now?'

Alex felt warm colour fill her cheeks. 'Well, that would be a good idea,' she said, giving a self-conscious laugh. 'That would make things easier all round, wouldn't it?'

He gave a wry smile. 'You'll find I don't surrender that easily.'

CHAPTER THREE

'I'M ALL done disturbing you, angel,' Callum murmured as the two-year-old girl fretted and tossed restlessly on the bed. 'No more horrible needles and stethoscopes and all that palaver.' He adjusted the medication drip, and then drew an ink line around the perimeter of the reddened area on the infant's leg. 'Let's hope that rash starts to shrink very soon,' he commented to the nurse who was assisting him. 'We'll make arrangements to admit her.'

He gave his attention back to the child. 'I think you'll be feeling a lot better before too long. I'm going to come back later to take a look at you, and I hope I'll find that nasty red area is beginning to disappear.' He carefully adjusted the bedcovers around the child, and gently brushed away the flaxen curls that massed around her hot cheeks. 'Just you go to sleep and let the medicine do its work. We'll have you right as rain in no time at all.'

Alex stood in the doorway of the treatment room, following his movements as he briefly checked the monitors. She had slipped into the room quietly, not wanting to disturb him, so he hadn't realised she was there, and for a moment or two she was able to watch him at work, undisturbed. It gave her a fascinating glimpse of the man behind the professional mask, and though she felt guilty at not announcing her presence, the compulsion to feast her gaze on him somehow overcame everything else.

He might well be a constant source of frustration to her where her budget schedule was concerned, but there was no doubting his commitment to the patients in his care. And even though paediatrics wasn't his specialty, she could see he had a sure instinct for dealing with children. This wasn't the first time she'd seen him tending to a youngster in A and E. It was clear that he had a genuine concern for his young charges, and the tenderness that she saw in him as he leaned over the cot brought an unexpected lump to her throat.

It made it all the more difficult that she had to confront him right now, but she had a job to do, regardless, and so she stiffened her shoulders and quietly claimed his attention. 'Might I have a word with you, please, Callum?' she said.

'Uh-oh...' Callum glanced at her, and then moved away from his young patient's bedside, giving final instructions to the nurse before walking towards the door where Alex waited, chart in hand. 'I've heard you use that tone of voice before...' he said under his breath, as he went out into the corridor. 'Quiet but insistent.' He frowned. 'It generally means I'm in trouble of some kind.'

'Not at all,' Alex murmured, following him and adding sweetly, 'You're obviously developing a persecution complex of some sort.'

He nodded, a faint grin tugging at his mouth. 'True. Funnily enough, it seemed to happen right about the time you joined the department.'

She tilted her head to one side. 'Guilty conscience, perhaps?'

He shook his head. 'Not true. I'm innocent as the day…at least, I think I am.' He glanced at the chart she was carrying. 'I expect that's one of mine, or you wouldn't be here. So what have I done this time?'

'It isn't just you,' Alex said in a sympathetic tone. 'I'm not singling you out. Please don't think that. I'm checking everyone's lab work to see if we can cut down on unnecessary testing… and here, looking at yours, I find you've ordered blood cultures, urine samples, swabs, to name just a few, for one small patient. Are you sure all these are really needed? Apart from the cost, we're laying a great strain on the laboratory facilities.'

He put on a stern face. 'If I hadn't needed them, I wouldn't have ordered them.'

'For a simple fever?'

'For a not-so-simple fever. The child was burning up, there was the beginning of a rash, and I suspect an insect bite of some sort that has led to a generalised infection which could lead to septicaemia.' He studied her. 'Do you really expect me to treat my patients without the proper diagnostic tools in place?'

'Of course not.' She smiled. 'I'm just checking, that's all. There's nothing wrong in making sure everyone keeps efficiency and cost awareness in the forefront of their mind, is there?'

He gave her a sour look. 'I'd appreciate it if you would take your checks elsewhere. I'm a consultant, remember, like yourself. I didn't get to this position by not knowing what I'm doing.'

'And I'm not suggesting otherwise. I see no reason why you should be so uptight about the situation,' she commented in a soothing tone, trying to placate him. 'We all want to do our best for our patients, and all I'm saying is that it's only natural that sometimes we might be a little over-zealous in our efforts.'

'I was not being over-zealous...I was being thorough. The child needs admission to hospital and treatment with an intravenous antibiotic. And if that doesn't meet with your approval, then I'm afraid it's too bad. That's how it's going to be.'

She put up a hand as though to ward him off. 'I'm not stopping you from doing anything. All

I'm saying is that we all have to be responsible and think carefully about the tests we order. It's easy to slip into lax ways when you're not the one counting the cost. Unfortunately, that's down to me, and ultimately I have the job of making sure everyone complies with the new, stringent measures.'

He gave her a long look. 'It never ceases to amaze me how very single-minded you are. Don't you ever relax and watch the world go by without wanting to leap on its back and wrestle it into shape?'

She gave him a bewildered glance. 'I've a job to do. What do you expect?'

'I expect you to take a breather every once in a while.' He checked the gold watch on his wrist, and as he moved she noticed the sprinkling of dark hairs that ran along his bare forearm. His shirtsleeves were rolled back, to show an expanse of skin that was lightly bronzed. His arms were muscular, his wrists strong, giving the impression of overwhelming masculinity, and for a second or two she felt a sudden tide of awareness that surged throughout her body and left her momentarily breathless.

He began to speak again, his voice cutting into her thoughts, and she reluctantly dragged her gaze away. It was strange, these weird sensations of being out of control that had afflicted her of late. She wasn't used to feeling this way. Perhaps she was overworked, stressed, and the sheer amount of changes that were taking place in her life right now was making her unduly sensitive.

'It's getting late,' he said, 'and I don't suppose you've had a break since lunchtime. I certainly haven't. Why don't we take a few minutes to go and get a cup of coffee—in my office, perhaps?'

She shook her head. 'I'm sorry,' she answered abruptly, struggling to get a grip on herself, 'but I don't have time. I have to finish this data chart by the end of my shift, and I'm already running late.'

'We could use the time to go over the budget cuts you had in mind,' he suggested silkily, a glint coming into his blue eyes. 'Of course, if you'd rather leave it until another day, that's fine by me.' He started to turn away.

Alex was suspicious of his sudden apparent willingness to work with her, but his offer was one she could hardly refuse, was it? 'Uh…maybe I was a little hasty. I dare say I could spare a few minutes, since you appear to have had a change of heart.'

'Change of heart? Me? I've always been happy to go along with your suggestions.'

She gave him a withering look. 'Let's not push it, shall we?'

He laughed softly, and stopped for a moment to sign off his patient's treatment chart before dropping it into a tray on the reception desk. 'Are there any casualty cards for me to fill in?' he asked the girl behind the counter.

She checked, but then a moment later shook her head. 'Seems you're all up to date,' she told him.

Callum gave Alex a smug glance. 'See?' he said. 'Didn't I say I was only too happy to work with you?'

She made a wry smile. 'I heard you'd shut yourself in your office and barred all callers after your shift yesterday so that you could catch up with things.' He hadn't been in the best of moods, by all accounts. 'Amazing what a little gentle badgering will do, isn't it?'

He huffed, and gently but firmly took her by the arm, and ushered her into his office. He shut the door.

'Oh my!' she exclaimed softly, looking around. 'You've done well for yourself, landing a prize room like this, haven't you? It's much bigger than mine.' She gazed out of the large, Georgian-style window onto a wooded landscape to the side of the hospital. 'What a beautiful view.' After a moment, she turned back to face him. 'I'd find it really hard to work in here—I'd be so distracted by that lovely scenery.'

'I was going to say, hands off,' he said thoughtfully, 'but maybe we should do a swap—it might help to slow you down a bit. I've never met anyone before who was so driven—well, maybe one, but she was an exception, like you.'

'You'd give up your room for me?' She seized on his words and stared at him, wide-eyed, ready to tease him mercilessly. 'What a lovely idea.' She gazed around the room once more, her glance taking in the glass-fronted bookcase and luxuriously upholstered leather chair. She ran her fingers lightly over the polished surface of his desk. 'I could really see me making myself at home in here.'

'Yes, so can I.' He watched her float dreamily about the room, stopping only to perch on the corner of the desk, draping herself possessively over it, one hand flat on the shiny top, the other resting lightly on her hip, her long legs crossed at the knee and showing a hint of creamy thigh. He looked at her abstractedly for a moment or two and appeared to be struggling to pull himself together.

'On second thoughts, forget it,' he said, going over to the other side of the room and setting out a bowl of sugar on the worktop. He retrieved a small jug of cream from the fridge. A coffee jug had been simmering gently on its base since they'd entered the room, but now he lifted it and began to pour the liquid into two mugs. 'I can just imagine,' he added in a droll tone, 'once you get yourself established in here, you'd be so invigorated you'll end up doing twice the amount of work you're doing now.'

She chuckled. 'You think so?'

'I know it.' He waved her to a padded leather chair by the side of the desk, and pushed the mug of coffee towards her. 'Help yourself to cream and sugar.'

'Thanks. Mmm…this is good.' She sniffed the aroma appreciatively and then went to sit down. 'Much better than the stuff in the machines out there.' She waved a hand towards the corridor outside and then frowned. 'But I'm a little concerned about your opinion of me. Where did you learn to be so mistrustful?'

His mouth quirked. 'At my mother's knee. And through dealing with people like you who prod and poke and instigate changes until what was once a smooth-running organisation becomes a mere sliver of what it was before.' He lifted his mug to his lips and swallowed the hot coffee. 'What is it that makes you so focussed and determined?'

She shrugged lightly, adding cream to her coffee

and stirring it slowly. 'I suppose I've always had a strong work ethic. It probably comes from my father. He believes in hard work, sticking to a task—for him there's no such word as "can't". He says there's always a solution and we have to keep going until we find it.'

'And you live by his rules, even now, even though you're a grown woman, with a mind of your own?'

'Why wouldn't I?' She met his gaze full on. 'It seems a reasonable enough philosophy to me. Besides, I've worked hard to get where I am today, and I'm not about to let it all slide. I always wanted to be a doctor...ever since I was little and I saw my friend being struck down by appendicitis, I knew it was the career for me. Now I've reached the point where I can see things that would be better for being changed, and I'm glad I'm in a position to do something about it.'

He sighed. 'Lord save us from a woman on a mission,' he murmured, his gaze sweeping over her. 'Does it never occur to you to stop for a while and look at things from someone else's viewpoint?'

'Like yours, you mean?' She shook her head. 'I've a feeling you think everything can stay the same, and you go ploughing on, regardless of the warnings from all around you. There'll come a time when the plough will break down and there will be no money to replace it. What will you do then?'

'Get a spade and start digging.' He frowned, studying her closely. 'I must say you seem to be very clinical in your attitude, and strangely un-emotional.'

She shrugged. 'Someone has to be.' She took another sip of her coffee and looked him over. His dark hair was a perfect foil for his rugged good looks and his eyes had that quality of being able to see right into your soul. It was disturbing, to say the least.

'Anyway,' she said, 'I've noticed the same work ethic in you. You put in a lot of hours, you're very dedicated to the job, and you must have been ambitious to get as far as you have in this profession. There aren't too many consultants around who are in their mid-thirties.' Her glance ran over him, gliding over the strong line of his jaw, coming to rest on the firmly moulded mouth that hinted at hidden sensuality. Dreamily, she wondered what it would be like to kiss him… Then she brought herself up sharply, veering away from the errant path her thoughts would have taken her. What on earth was wrong with her?

'I suppose that's true.' He looked at her oddly, as though he was trying to fathom what was going on in her mind, and a wave of heat ran through her body. Heaven forbid he should work it out!

'So what made you decide to become a doctor?' she asked. 'Are your parents in the same line of work? You said they were working with under-privileged children.'

He nodded. 'In a manner of speaking, they are. They're part of the World Health Organization, so mostly their work involves organising medical care. They generally manage to collaborate with one another on various projects.'

'So I guess you don't see much of them?'

'That's true. Of course, they come home on vacation, and they have a fairly generous span of time off, but they're dedicated to what they do, especially my mother. The job is very important to her.'

He gave a faint smile but didn't comment any further, and Alex was prompted to ask, 'Would I be right in thinking your mother is the other person you know who is "driven", as you put it?'

'I guess so.' He pressed his lips together briefly. 'She's a very fierce believer in getting things done. Once she sets her mind on doing something, it becomes the be-all and end-all...there's no stopping her. Of course, that's great, if you've a project that needs to be up and running, but it doesn't bode well for anyone who would hanker after a cosy home life.'

'Like you?' She was frowning a little, wondering what it must have been like for him as a young child to live with parents who were constantly travelling the world. 'I expect you must have seen more than your fair share of countries.'

'That's right. I always went with them in the beginning, but there came a time when I was due to start my secondary education, and I wanted stability. So that's where my aunt and uncle came in…although my uncle passed away a few years ago. My parents kept in touch by phone and email—we even have a video link set up now.' He smiled. 'My mother was anxious about leaving me, but Aunt Jane is a home bird and she more than made up for any sense of loss I might be feeling. My uncle and aunt didn't have any children of their own, and so I think they were glad of the chance to look after me.'

'She's a lovely woman,' Alex said. 'I took to her straight away—and the minute she saw that I had children she offered to help out. I still feel anxious about letting her take that on, especially with the school holidays coming up soon…but she seemed like a godsend at the time.'

He nodded. 'Strange, that,' he murmured. 'I'd no idea that you had children.' He stood up then to go and fetch biscuits from a cupboard on the wall. 'We have bourbons, sandwich creams, plain, ginger…' he said, rummaging through the various packets. 'Or there are fruited tea buns left over from yesterday afternoon.' He pressed the packaging to test their freshness, and his features lit up. 'They seem fine. Would you like one?'

She grinned at his boyish pleasure. 'Thanks, that would be great.'

He set them out on plates, and added a selection of biscuits. 'I'm starving,' he told her with a hint of apology. 'My lunch was interrupted today—an emergency cropped up. It's always happening—that's why I keep a stash of goodies on hand in here.'

He came to sit back down, and pushed a plate towards her before biting into a tea bun. 'You'll be pleased to know that I made an appointment for my aunt to see a specialist friend of mine—I managed to arrange it for next week, so we should soon know the score about what's causing the high blood pressure. Like you, I've been worried about her.'

'I'm glad you did that.' Alex smiled, and he looked at her, almost as though he was seeing her for the first time, his gaze lingering on her features for a while.

Then he seemed to pull himself together and said cautiously, 'As I said, it was a bit of a shock to find that you had children. It must make things difficult for you, doing a high-powered job like this one and still having to maintain a family life.'

'It isn't easy, I grant you.' Alex took a bite from the remaining bun, and chewed thoughtfully for a moment or two. 'First there was the move down here to Somerset, that was an ordeal in itself, for me, at least, and it was a bit of a challenge for the children, having to settle into a new house.'

He glanced at the fingers of her left hand, and then frowned. 'And your husband? I don't see a ring. Are you and he divorced…separated?'

'Neither. I've never been married.' She finished off the bun.

He drew in a deep breath and looked faintly puzzled. 'But the children's father…'

'Is in hospital. He's my brother.' She took pity on his bewilderment and went on, 'He and my sister-in-law were involved in a bad motorway accident. They were travelling back from a reception organised by his firm when it happened, so, in one way, perhaps it was fortunate that they were on their own in the car. The children were staying with friends.'

'I'm so sorry, Alex.' He reached for her hand,

covering it with his palm. 'That must have been a terrible shock for you.'

'Yes, it was.' She tried not to think about the way his gentle touch evoked warm ripples of sensation and sent them coursing along the length of her arm. 'I suppose, in the end, I'm just thankful that they survived. It was bad, but it could have been worse.'

'Yes, it could. But at least the children were safe. I suppose that became the immediate priority.'

She nodded. She was finding it hard to concentrate with his long fingers clasping hers. It was a gesture of comfort and support, and it made her feel good inside, as though he was letting her know he was there for her and that she need not be alone in all this. It had been a long while since she'd felt that way.

'There was no one to look after the children, and Beth was desperate that they shouldn't go into care, so I stepped in. I love my family and I want to do the best for them.'

'Of course you do.' He frowned. 'So what was the reason for you buying the house?' he asked in a puzzled tone. 'Didn't they have a place of their own?'

'They did. They'd all moved into rented accommodation some six months ago when Ross took up a new job in the area, but the lease expired and the landlord didn't want to renew it. So I had to look for a place with enough room for all of us.'

He shook his head. 'It sounds as though you had a hefty task on your hands. I can't imagine having to juggle all those problems at once. You must have worked wonders to hold it all together.'

She gave him a faint smile. 'I don't know about holding it all together. Sometimes I worry that I've taken on too much, especially with the house. But at least the children were already settled at school. That was one less problem to sort out.' Her brows drew together. 'All I have to worry about now are the school holidays. I'm going to have to sort out some full-time care for them. I don't want to ask Jane, because she seems so unwell.'

'That's true, but I'm sure you'll find someone very capable and willing to look after them. Obviously it will be better if it's someone you know.'

He frowned. 'And this job must be an extra worry for you. You've taken on a big responsibility.'

She sighed. 'Yes, but I'm sure things could work out well if we just put our heads together and try to sort things out...' she sucked in a breath '...which reminds me, weren't we going to discuss those budget cuts?'

'It's true, we were.' He straightened up, reluctantly sliding his hand away from her. Then he swallowed the remains of his coffee and glanced down at his pager. 'But it appears that I'm wanted in Resus.' He glanced at her. 'Sorry to have to break things up, but I must go.'

Alex stared at him. 'I didn't hear your pager go off.'

'No,' he said, 'you wouldn't. I set it to silent alarm.' He showed her the text message that was displayed on the pager's screen and then gave her an encouraging smile. 'But not to worry, perhaps we can do this another day? I'll come up with all the figures you want, I promise. Meanwhile, why don't you stay here and finish your coffee? It's been good to see you relax for a while. I'm sure a little longer will do you the world of good.'

He stood up and made for the door, and Alex was filled with frustration as she watched his disappearing back. It seemed that all her efforts to get the job done were fated where he was concerned.

CHAPTER FOUR

'IF ONE more ball goes flying over the fence into next door's garden, I shall stop you from playing football out there.' Alex abandoned her battle with the ancient Aga and went to remonstrate with James in the garden. 'Auntie Jane has better things to do than to keep throwing them back, and sooner or later you're going to damage something.'

'Oops.' The warning came too late. James pulled a face as his favourite football went sailing over the fence and was followed a second or two later by an ominous thudding sound. 'I didn't mean it,' he said, with a bemused expression. 'It was an accident.'

Alex sighed. 'You'd better go round there and apologise,' she told him. Turning to his sister, she said, 'Will you go with him, Sarah, please? Find out if there's been any damage. I have to stay here and keep an eye on the pizza in the oven.'

'Okay.' Sarah took James by the hand and led him away.

'Why do we have to go?' James complained. 'I didn't do it on purpose. I just tapped it and it went over.'

'Yeah, like always,' Sarah said. 'That's 'cos you keep trying to see how high you can kick it.'

'No…I was just aiming for the goal. You wanna see how Rooney does it,' James said, warming to his theme. 'See how they did it in the match on telly? You have to run and shoot, get it in there quick.'

'Yeah, but they lost the game,' Sarah pointed out in a blunt tone. 'Didn't do them any good, did it?'

'Well, they'll do it next time.' James scowled at his sister as they went out of the back gate.

Alex could still hear them bickering as they walked along the path to her neighbour's property. A wave of guilt swamped her. There was no doubt about it, she ought to have gone with them, but there was just so much to do…lunch to prepare, laundry to finish, ironing, and that was before she made a start on tackling the endless round of decorating that was needed to spruce up this old farmhouse property.

And now the Aga was playing up. The pizza, which should have been cooked several minutes ago, was still pale looking, and Alex guessed that meant she would soon be paying out for a new thermostat for the oven.

She left it to bake some more and started to gather together the ingredients for a salad. And what of the football game that had gone wrong out there? Was she going to have to fork out for damage to Jane's property as well?

The children came back a few minutes later. 'Auntie Jane made us a cake,' Sarah said excitedly, bursting into the kitchen.

'Goodness! A reward for causing her all that trouble? Auntie Jane must be a saint.'

'It's all covered with strawberries and cream.' James was licking his lips in anticipation. 'I'm hungry,' he said. 'Can we have some now?'

'After you've eaten your lunch,' Alex murmured.

'Isn't that just typical of adults?' a familiar, deep voice commented, and Alex was startled to see Callum follow the children into the kitchen. 'There are never any goodies to be had till after the main course, are there?' He peered around the door. 'Is it all right if I come in?' His glance slid warmly over her, moving from head to toe and taking in her slender shape, outlined by the snug-fitting jeans and the stretchy cotton top she wore.

'Of course.' She studied him in return, flummoxed for a moment, seeing him here, in her kitchen. He looked good, dressed in casual clothes, dark chinos teamed with a loose cotton shirt, a strong contrast to the smart, formal suits he wore for work.

She waved him to a seat by the table. 'Come and sit down.' She frowned, and then added hesitantly, 'I was just about to serve up lunch. You're welcome to stay and eat with us, if you like.'

He smiled, seeming surprised by the invitation, and she was back-footed all over again by the way the smile softened his angular features.

'Are you sure? Thanks. That would be great...if you're positive it's no trouble?'

'None at all...though I won't guarantee the state of the pizza.' She frowned. 'It started out with all the promise of a healthy, home-made meal, but it's a bit of a sorry effort now, given that the Aga's putting on a go-slow.' She took the pizza from the oven and set it out on the worktop.

Callum studied it. 'Looks fine to me. Lovely golden melted cheese...with ham, tomato and salami... Definitely a winner.' He sniffed the air appreciatively. 'Smells good, too. This reminds me of being in my aunt's kitchen when I was young. Lots of lovely baking smells.'

'Talking of which...' He held out a large, round plastic container and placed it on the table. 'Aunt Jane asked me to give you this...it's her famous Somerset pound cake. Apparently it's a mix of butter, sugar, flour and a whole basket full of eggs.' He grinned. 'I can tell you from experience that it's a mouth-watering concoction, anyway.'

Alex looked at the cake. 'It's wonderful,' she said. 'She's too good to us—we really don't deserve it after the trouble we've been to her. I've lost count of the number of times the ball has landed in her vegetable patch—and last time it went over, we heard this awful thud…was anything broken?'

He shook his head. 'The shed took a strong hit, but it's a solid, sturdy piece of workmanship. She says not to worry about it.'

'That's easier said than done. I'd be getting stressed out if the neighbours kept doing it to me.'

His mouth made an odd quirk. 'Yes, but you seem to be constantly under pressure, what with work and keeping up with this place. Aunt Jane tells me you're finding all sorts of problems here—you need to have some of the roof tiles replaced, she says. That must be a hassle you can do without.'

'And the rest.' She pulled a face. 'I didn't realise this place needed quite so much work, when I took it on.' She glanced at him as she set out plates on the table. 'But you must be having problems of your own—didn't you say you had builders working on your house? It was why you hadn't been able to get around to seeing your aunt, you said.'

'That's right. I was having work done on the garage and in the garden. The work's all finished now, though. Obviously, it was nothing compared with what you have to do here.'

Alex nodded. 'I keep asking myself why I bought this place.' She broke off to tell James and Sarah to go and wash their hands at the sink. 'Originally, I'd no intention of buying such a rambling place, but it sort of drew me in... It looked like a dream house, with its lovely, honey-coloured Somerset stone and the sloping roofs at all angles, and once I set eyes on it, I was hooked. I've never owned a house before...I've always lived in small, rented accommodation. Nothing else seemed necessary.'

'But suddenly you wanted to put down roots?'

She nodded. 'I think so. I don't know why. I really don't know what came over me. Up to now, I've been so busy with work that I didn't need anything more than a place to rest my head. Then I came here...' She frowned. 'Perhaps I thought it was time for a change. I had visions of this old farmhouse being lovingly renovated, and the orchard bursting with fruit—a kind of rural paradise, if you like.' She grinned. 'Now I'm beginning to wonder if I might have bitten off more than I can chew.'

Callum opened his mouth to answer, but he was interrupted by a horrible clanking and groaning sound coming from the water pipes as the children turned on the kitchen tap. No water came out.

'Where's the spanner?' James asked, his face serious as he began to hunt around in the cupboard underneath the sink.

'Isn't it there?' Alex frowned. 'I must have moved it. Look on the shelf by the fridge.'

Callum looked from one to the other, clearly puzzled. 'He's not going to try to fix it, is he? Surely he's too young?'

'Nah…it's easy,' James told him, putting on his man-of-the-house expression. He found the spanner and bent down inside the cupboard, concentrating deeply on the task in hand. Then he gave the pipe a couple of hard whacks. 'Try it now,' he instructed Sarah.

She did as he told her, and obligingly water spurted from the tap.

Callum watched in wonder. 'I'm impressed. Who needs a tradesman when you can do it yourself?'

Alex's mouth curved. 'It is annoying, though,' she said. 'The water pipes creak and groan and make an almighty noise a lot of the time. I'm going to have to do something about it, because one of these days banging on the pipe just won't do the trick.'

The children finished washing and came to sit at the table. 'I love pizza,' James said, trying to cram a whole portion into his mouth at once.

'That's great, but slow down,' Alex warned him. 'I don't want to see you choking on your food.'

James grinned amiably, and he and Sarah compared slices before James began to show his sister how to make faces with pieces he arranged carefully on his plate. 'You just cut it with your knife, like this,' he explained.

Alex turned her attention to Callum. 'So how is Jane?' she asked. 'I looked in on her this morning, but it seemed as though she'd been overdoing things again. Her cheeks were very flushed, and

I guessed her blood pressure was up. Has there been any news from the hospital?'

'Yes, I talked to the specialist yesterday, and I gave her the news this afternoon. She said it was okay to let you know the result.'

'And that is?'

'She has Conn's syndrome. It's very rare, and that's perhaps why it wasn't picked up before, but the CT scan showed a tumour on her adrenal gland. It's causing the gland to produce too much aldosterone, and that's pushing up her blood pressure.'

Alex pressed her lips together briefly. 'That must have come as a huge shock to her. Is she all right?'

'I think so. She went to lie down for a while, but she seemed to take it well enough.'

'And what about you? How do you feel about it? It must be a real worry for you.'

His mouth straightened. 'I'm not sure. Generally these things turn out to be benign, so I'm trying to stay calm about it. I tried to paint a positive picture for my aunt, too…but she's a hardy woman, generally. I think she'll be all right. Things don't normally knock her back for long.'

Alex pulled in a quick breath. 'I'll make sure to give her any help and support she needs,' she vowed. 'When will she be having the surgery? Is your friend going to operate?'

He nodded. 'He said he'd do it next week. One of his patients postponed, because of unexpected travel plans, so he'll fit my aunt in then.'

'That's brilliant news. She's healthy enough otherwise, isn't she, so there shouldn't be any problem?'

'Let's hope so.' He helped himself to salad, and then sent a cautious glance in the children's direction before asking quietly, 'How are your family doing? You said they were involved in a nasty accident and they must already have been in hospital for quite a while.'

Her eyes clouded. 'It's going to take some time before they're back on their feet. Ross is still on a ventilator, but Beth is doing a little better. Even so, there were broken bones that need to heal, as well as the internal injuries.'

She shot a look at the children. Thankfully,

they were both still engrossed in seeing who could make the best pattern with what was left of the pizza. Sarah had added cherry tomatoes to her effort, along with a curved slice of red pepper for a mouth, and now she pronounced that she had made the best face.

'She has curly hair, too,' she said proudly, showing off the adornment of pasta spirals.

James pursed his lips. 'Faces are easy,' he said. 'I'm making a tractor.'

'Oh, is that what it is?' Sarah squinted at his effort, tilting her head sideways so as to see it from a different angle. 'You need some salami rings for the wheels.'

'Yes, but I ate them,' James said, frowning. He inspected her plate. 'Can I have yours?'

'No, you can't.' Sarah moved her plate out of reach when he would have swooped with his fork, and Alex closed her eyes fleetingly.

'Try eating your food instead of playing with it. And when you've finished, you can go outside and play on the swing for a while. Get rid of some of that energy,' Alex said to both of them.

'I want to play football,' James said, his grey eyes challenging her.

'No more football today,' she answered. 'We talked about that.'

'Well, then, why can't we go to the seaside instead? You keep saying we'll go, but we never do.'

'Yes, but we've only been here a few weeks, James, and we've been busy. There's been a lot to do, moving in here and getting everything shipshape.'

'It isn't a ship!' James retorted, his brows shooting upwards. 'I want to go to the seaside.' He glowered. 'Mum would have taken us.'

Alex hid a groan, and Callum's mouth twitched a fraction. 'They know how to hit where it hurts, don't they?'

'Too right they do.' She glanced at the children, but by now James was making another attempt to steal salami from Sarah's plate, and she decided it was time to intervene.

She picked up James's plate and held it aloft. 'Have you finished with this?' she asked. 'Do you want me to put this out for the birds?'

James scowled, but shook his head.

'All right, then. Eat up. Any more messing about and I'll take it away, and then there'll be no strawberry cake.'

Both children began to eat, and Alex gave a faint sigh. 'They're like this all the while,' she told Callum, with a shake of her head. 'I don't know how their mother used to cope. I feel as though I'm run ragged half the time, sorting out their disputes.'

'I expect she lets them get on with it,' he said, smiling. 'By the time you've come around to playing referee, they'll have moved on to something else.'

'That's true enough,' she said with a laugh.

He glanced at the youngsters, who had begun to argue over which one of them had more cheese than the other, and added softly, 'Of course, James does have a point about the seaside, you know. To a child, a day can seem a long while to wait for something, let alone several weeks—and the coast is only a few miles from here.'

A small line creased her brow. 'I know I should have taken them—it's just that the weekends are so full, and they haven't really mentioned it much.'

'Perhaps they were waiting for you to arrange it. Anyway, I can't help sympathising with youngsters who want to spend time at the seaside… especially when their parents aren't around to take them there.'

'I know.' She frowned. 'I kept thinking we'd wait until I have some time off from work, in the summer holidays. As it is, I have a mass of work to do here. I'm halfway through painting the living room, I have to do something about the blocked-up chimney in the dining room, and the kitchen cupboards need stripping down to bare wood so that they can be restored to what they once were. And that's not counting the roof tiles that need replacing and the plumbing that needs to be fixed. I just don't know when I'm supposed to do all this.'

'Later,' he said. 'All those things can wait. You need to get your priorities sorted out.'

'Do I?' She made a soft sound of exasperation. 'That's easy for you to say, isn't it? You're not involved. As far as I can tell, everything's going smoothly for you, and all you have to do is make sure your aunt is safe and secure.'

'Maybe, but I'd like to do what I can to help you. I'm sure we can find a solution.'

'What do you mean?'

'I mean how about I take a look at the plumbing, while you clear the table and get everyone ready for a trip to the coast? I know a lovely little cove not far from here, where the children can fish in the rock pools.'

'Yes!'

'Yes!'

Alex looked round in astonishment as James and Sarah both shouted gleefully, whooping with delight. 'Say yes, Auntie Alex…please say yes.' Sarah turned pleading blue eyes on Alex, and James's face was lit up with joyful expectation.

Alex was stunned to find that they had both been listening to her conversation with Callum. She turned to him. 'Now look what you've done.'

Callum's expression was bland. 'Who? Me? I didn't do anything. I just offered to try and fix the taps for you. If you want me to leave it, that's fine by me.'

'No, no…Auntie Alex, don't let him leave it…' Sarah was beside herself with dismay. 'You keep saying how you're going to…knock that pipe into next week if it doesn't stop playing up. Now you don't have to. I know he can fix it for us…or at least he can try.'

'And then we can go to the seaside,' James finished.

'Yeah!' They both added the chorus.

Alex melted at the sight of the children's eager faces. 'I don't see how I have any choice.' She looked at Callum and gave a faint shake of her head. 'There are a thousand and one jobs I should be doing, but now it looks as though I'll be spending the afternoon by the sea.' She gave him a mischievous look. 'Maybe you could help out in other ways,' she suggested with a wry smile. 'Perhaps you'd like to come and do my laundry while you're about it, and mop the floors?'

His mouth twisted. 'Sorry, but I don't do domestic. I come from a household steeped in tradition—Aunt Jane did all the homely things, and my uncle ran the show from his study. He always had lots of advice on how things should be done…but leave it to the women, he used to say.'

Her mouth curved. 'Well, let's hope at least you can fix the plumbing,' she said. 'That would be a definite bonus.'

He nodded. 'I'll need a carrier bag and a sponge of some sort if you have one?'

She stared at him blankly. 'Those aren't the usual plumbing tools, are they? I can offer you spanners, a wrench, hammers…pliers or grips…'

'A carrier bag and sponge will be just fine, thanks… and some plastic adhesive tape if you have it.'

She frowned. 'Okay.' She studied him briefly. 'Are you quite sure you know what you're doing?'

He nodded. 'I hope so.'

She went to fetch him what he needed, and then sent the children upstairs to get ready for their outing. 'You'll need a spare set of clothes in case anything gets wet,' she told them. 'And you'd better hunt out your swimsuit and trunks.'

'Seaside! Yay!' James ran up the stairs, followed swiftly by Sarah. 'Can we take the fishing nets?' he called back.

'I'll get them,' Alex told him. She stopped to think about that for a moment or two. Last time she'd seen them, they'd been at the back of the shed, along with buckets and spades from previous years...years when they'd gone with their parents to spend time by the sea, digging in the sand and making spectacular sandcastles, with moats and drawbridges, and all sorts of embellishments made from shells and pebbles that they'd found lying about. She'd seen the photos, and heard all about it from Ross and Beth.

The memories brought sudden tears to her eyes. How could she ever hope to replace all that love and commitment, even for a short time? Would things be the same for them ever again?

'Are you all right?' Callum was looking at her oddly, and Alex blinked, trying to stem the tears that threatened.

'I'm fine,' she said, her voice a little choked. 'I was just thinking about Ross and Beth...it caught me unawares. I suppose I've been a bit wound up lately, trying to work out how to deal with everything.'

He wrapped his arms around her and drew her

close. 'You're bound to feel that way,' he said softly. 'So much has happened in such a short time.' He ran his hands over her shoulders, her back, gently soothing her.

'I'm just afraid I've let them down.' Her voice faltered. 'It's as though I've been suffering from tunnel vision lately, trying to form order out of chaos. I've concentrated so hard on dealing with day-to-day life…it all seemed so important at the time.'

He rested his cheek against hers. 'Perhaps it was the only way you could cope. But what really matters is that they should be happy. You can't make up for this awful thing that has struck down their parents, but you can do something to help the children.'

She nodded. 'You're right. I know you're right.'

He smiled. 'Anyway, you could do with a break yourself. It's time to step off the treadmill—so, if you'll pass me the sponge and tape, I'll get on.'

He carefully released her, easing back from her a little, and she took a moment to get used to being on her own once again. She missed his warm embrace. She missed his closeness.

But she needed to pull herself together, so she went to find the things he needed.

She handed them to him a minute or so later, and then watched curiously as he placed the sponge inside the carrier bag and taped it firmly beneath the outlet of the tap.

'First we switch on the cold tap,' he said, 'then the hot. Wait for the gurgling to stop…then turn off the hot tap.' He waited a moment or two, leaving the cold tap running, and then abruptly removed the bag and sponge. Water spurted out.

'We'll try that one or two times more,' he murmured, 'and see if it does the trick. It's just an airlock that's causing the trouble.'

A minute or two later, the water was running freely, and Alex watched and marvelled. 'Thank you for that,' she said. 'I would never have guessed it was something so simple. I can see I'm going to have to get myself a book on how to fix things around the house…or find a decent internet site that explains everything in layman's terms.'

'As opposed to having a man around the place?' He sent her an oblique glance, a smile playing around his lips. 'Are you sure you wouldn't prefer your own handyman on the premises?'

Her mouth curved. 'Are you putting yourself forward for the job?'

'Oh, yes.' His glimmering gaze skimmed over her. 'With perks, of course…'

'Oh?' She looked at him warily. 'And they would be?'

'Well, let's see…you could pay me with tea and pizza, or maybe a slice of strawberry cream cake…'

'That sounds reasonable enough,' she said with a smile. 'I think we could manage both of those.'

'Hmm.' He dried his hands on a tea towel and then turned to face her once more. 'Though there are other far more interesting ways I could think of.' His gaze lingered on the pink fullness of her mouth, and she simply stood there for a moment, lured by the sheer invitation in those incredible blue eyes and wondering what it would be like to be kissed by him. Somehow he was so close that it would only take a breath of movement, and his lips would be touching hers. She felt heady with the intensity of the moment, lulled by the spell he was weaving around her.

'James wants to take his snorkel and flippers,' Sarah said, coming into the kitchen at that moment. 'I told him we're not going swimming, but he won't listen. And he thinks we're going to take the dinghy and his wooden boat as well as the beach ball.'

Alex came back down to earth with a bump. She gave Callum one last, cautious glance, and saw that his mouth had curved into a resigned smile. 'Tell him the beach ball and his wooden boat are fine,' she said, trying to keep her voice on an even keel. 'And we'd better get a move on if we're to have plenty of time at the beach.'

She turned to Callum, breathing in deeply to calm herself. 'Will your aunt be okay while we're out? It seems like the wrong time to leave her.'

'I'm sure she'll be fine. Martha from across the way is coming over to visit her this afternoon, so at least she'll have company. Anyway, she knows to ring me if there's a problem…but I'll go and have a word with her right now, and then we'll set off.' He paused a moment, then added, 'You might want to ask Martha about looking after the children during the school holidays, if my aunt's going to be out of action for a while. She used to foster children, so I know she'd like the opportunity.'

'Really? That's great. I'll talk to her about it.' She marvelled at his thoughtfulness. She'd been trying to work out what to do for the best, and he had come up with a solution. Having him around was turning out to be a boon.

'Good. And as to what we were saying before… I'll come round and give you a hand with some of the jobs you have to do around here. I'm quite handy with a paintbrush and I'm not too bad on fixing roof tiles either. Between us, we should soon have this place looking good.'

'Oh…that's really thoughtful of you.' The words left her on a soft breath of surprise and, impulsively, she reached out to touch his arm. 'That's a wonderful offer, but you don't need to do that. I took it on, and it's my problem. I'm the one who should deal with it.'

'I don't see it as a problem. I see it as a project. I'll be really glad of the chance to help you renovate this place on my days off. It'll be good to have something to do that's completely different from work at the hospital.' He smiled as he walked towards the door. 'And it will give us the chance to spend more time together.'

She stared at him in shock, stunned by his offer. Did he really want to spend his weekends with her?

By the time he came back from Jane's house, they were all ready to set off. James was wearing his super-spy slimline shades, and Sarah had her favourite drinks bottle with the curly plastic straw.

Callum drove along the main road towards the coast, pointing out the various landmarks along the way. Soon, the rolling hills of the Quantocks gave way to Exmoor's rugged landscape, with majestic headlands, towering cliffs and beautiful bays. The sea was a perfect blue.

'I thought we'd stop at a little cove near here,' he said, as he turned the car onto a road leading towards the sea. 'It's sheltered by the cliffs, so you can get some shade from the sun, and when the tide's out, as it is now, it leaves behind lots of pools where you can find baby crabs.'

He parked the car and looked back at James. 'Did you bring a bucket?'

James nodded, holding up a huge blue bucket, shaped like a castle. 'For the crabs,' he said.

'Good. A boy after my own heart,' Callum said. He glanced at Sarah. 'Are you all right with crabbing? Not squeamish, are you?'

Sarah shook her head. 'But Auntie Alex isn't too keen. She doesn't like their little pincers.'

He laughed. 'I might have guessed.' He sent Alex a sympathetic look. 'Not to worry. You can collect shells and seaweed instead, if you like.'

'Thank you so much,' Alex answered, her tone dry. 'I can't think of anything I'd like more.'

He nodded. 'You will, once you get the hang of this "taking things easy" exercise.'

'Of course I will,' she murmured. 'I have vague memories of it, from when I was in my teens, I think.'

'What it is to be focussed,' he said softly. 'Is your career really the be-all and end-all of everything?'

They climbed out of the car, unloading rubber rings, a huge beach ball, the bag with towels and a change of clothes, and another bag with camera, drinks bottles and assorted paraphernalia.

'Do you remember good times by the sea with your parents?' Alex asked Callum as they walked down the cliff path to the sand below.

'Some,' he said. 'But mostly I went with Aunt Jane and my uncle. They'd let me bring a friend along, sometimes a couple of friends, and we had some great times.' He looked around. 'This was a favourite haunt.'

She nodded, looking around for a place where they could settle down when they reached the sandy beach. 'I can see why. It has everything you could want.'

She handed out buckets and spades, and the children set to work, digging in the sand. 'I'm going to make a fort,' James announced, 'with battlements and a moat.'

Alex gazed out over the sparkling waters of the Bristol Channel, and then looked back at the cliffs, layered with strata of shale, and blue, yellow and brown limestone. 'This place is fantastic.'

'It is,' Callum agreed. 'I used to hunt for fossils in those rocks. It was great fun.'

'I can imagine.'

They spent the next hour digging in the sand and fetching water from the sea so that James and Sarah could complete their grand castle. That done, they set off to explore the cove, treading carefully over flat rocks and peering down into rocky inlets where the tide had washed up all manner of seaweed and sea creatures.

James filled his bucket with baby crabs, while Sarah collected shells, looking for perfect specimens. 'I want to take them to the hospital to show Mum,' she said.

Alex watched as they padded over the damp sand. Callum bent to look at James's latest find, and the two males engaged in a deep discussion about how the creature moved and whether it could live out of water. Then Callum turned to Sarah and admired the perfectly intact cockleshell she had discovered.

He was good with both of them, Alex acknowledged. He spoke to them quietly, interested in everything they had to say, and every now and then his gentle laughter floated on the air.

Eventually, they returned to the sandcastle where they had started off, and Alex hunted out drinks from the depths of one of the bags. Satisfied after quenching his thirst, James wanted to go down to the water's edge to paddle in the surf.

'Okay, but stay where I can see you,' Alex told him. 'No further than that wooden marker.'

Sarah went with him, and Alex watched their progress, anxious in case they should wander too far into the water.

'It's a safe beach,' Callum told her. 'They'll be okay...and we'll both keep an eye on them.'

She nodded. 'This is really lovely, being out here. It seems so long since I last sat on a beach and looked at the sea. I didn't realise how much I missed it.'

'Didn't you take holidays?'

She shook her head. 'I haven't done recently. Somehow I just don't seem to have found time for a proper break these last few years. I've been studying for specialist exams, taking on high-profile jobs and generally letting myself be swamped with work.'

'I suppose you must get an adrenaline buzz from all that, otherwise you wouldn't do it.'

'Maybe.' Her eyes clouded. Why was it that her life's work suddenly seemed nothing compared to these stolen moments in a sandy cove where the only sounds were the gentle swish of the sea lapping at the shore and the call of the gulls overhead? What had she been missing all these years?

Callum leaned back against a rock and studied her with a quizzical expression. 'And where do men friends fit into all this hard work and dedication to the job in hand? You said you were too busy to be involved with anyone right now, but there must have been someone in the past?'

'Maybe.' She wasn't going to fill him in on her skirmishes with romance, and anyway it seemed odd to say that no man had ever featured greatly in her life. There had been opportunity enough, if she'd wanted to take it, but somehow no one had ever lit that spark in her that would make her fall head over heels in love. There had been good men, rugged men, men who'd made her laugh and promised her the world, but none had made her want to give up her career or turn her back on ambition. Perhaps there was something wrong with her. Perhaps she was expecting too much.

'I see…dark secrets, eh?' Callum tilted his head on one side to study her. 'I heard there was a doctor in Men's Surgical who lost his heart to you for quite a while. A couple of years, at least, but it was unrequited love, people said. They say you think more about the job than you do about your love life.' His glance meshed with hers. 'That's quite a challenge for any man.'

'Is it?' She saw his gaze drop to her mouth, and felt a sudden flood of heat in her abdomen. 'I don't know what to do about that, because the truth is I mean it when I say I don't have time for a relationship right now.' Her mouth made a brief quirk. 'Heavens, I don't even have time to do my ironing. At this rate, the children will be wearing crumpled T-shirts to school in the morning.'

He laughed. 'I don't suppose anyone will mind. You'll be the only one who notices.' He leaned over her and smoothed back a tendril of hair that had fallen across her cheek.

'Maybe. But that's the problem I'm wrestling with, isn't it? I notice all these things and I care about them, and I want to put them right. Not T-shirts so much, but generally taking care of the children and making sure everything runs smoothly.'

'It could be that these things aren't so important as you imagine.'

'But they matter to me.'

Perhaps that was the reason none of her relationships had worked out right in the past. She had her own set of priorities, and the men she had known had without fail wanted to override them with their own concerns. Callum was probably much the same.

She gazed out to sea, to where the children were splashing one another and jumping with each wave that rolled onto the shore. 'The tide's coming in,' she said. 'I think we'll have to make a move.'

'Yes.' There was a note of regret in his voice. 'I think you're probably right.'

CHAPTER FIVE

'YES, I understand perfectly, Dr Langton... we're looking for cuts right across the board.' Alex frowned. 'Of course, you realise, don't you, that it isn't as simple as cutting back on nursing staff and putting the cleaning contract out to tender? Either of those measures could mean that the emergency department will function less well.' Alex adopted a gentle, coaxing tone. 'I was hoping rather that we might make savings through using low-priced generic drugs and altering practices within the unit so that we're more cost-efficient.'

Dr Langton shook his head. 'My dear, that simply won't be enough. From the figures you've shown me, those measures will take far too long to bring results. Unfortunately, this job's all about tough decisions. We need to do something now... and reducing staff numbers is top priority, along with putting a stop on any new equipment being ordered. Some departments are quite irresponsible in thinking they can demand all the latest equipment…we simply don't have the budget for it.' He frowned. 'Make sure they know that in A and E, won't you? Out of all the departments, that one has the highest expenditure for the last six months.'

'I've already done that,' she said. 'I've put a stop to any new orders.'

'Good.' He gave her a benign smile. 'We need to show the board that we've made dramatic headway at the next meeting…but I know you can pull this off, Alex. I've every faith in you.'

Alex nodded. 'I'll do my best. At least with all these measures in place we should be able to keep the A and E department up and running. I've looked closely at the figures and everything seems to be on course.'

He nodded. 'That's what it's all about.'

She left the chief executive's office a short time later, deep in thought, and made her way to A and E. Things were going from bad to worse.

Right from the beginning, this day had started out wrong.

First of all she had visited Ross and Beth, only to find that her brother had suffered a setback. His breathing had deteriorated, and the doctors were worried about an infection in his lungs. They were initiating more tests and thinking about changing his medication...all of it bad news. How was she to explain things to the children? And on top of that, this was the day that Jane was having surgery to remove the tumour on her adrenal gland...one more thing to play on her mind.

For now, though, she tried to concentrate on the job in hand. She didn't have to look too far to find the culprit behind some of the so-called irresponsible ordering that had annoyed the chief executive.

Callum was determined that A and E should have the best equipment for the job, and although he was aware that the budget was restricted, he'd been determinedly pushing for those things he felt necessary.

And as for staff cuts, those wouldn't go down

well at all, would they? It was a disturbing situation. Even though Dr Langton was the boss, she couldn't help thinking he was being short-sighted in ordering them.

'There you are…I'm glad you're back from your meeting,' Katie greeted her as she entered the unit. 'We've a three-year-old in treatment room two—he has a foreign body in his ear, and so far Dr Henderson hasn't been able to remove it. The boy's getting quite distressed, and his mother's becoming agitated, too. Dr Henderson's tried irrigation and now he's having a go with forceps. He doesn't like to admit defeat and he's doing his level best, but I think it's a difficult one for him. He asked for a second opinion.'

'Okay, I'll go and see the boy. It's not easy dealing with youngsters when they're fractious, and it's amazing how deep into the ear canal they can push things.' She glanced at Katie. 'Is there a nurse assisting?'

Katie shook her head. 'No, everyone's busy at the moment, but I could go along if you like. I've finished here for the moment.'

'That would be great, if you would. He might need help to calm the infant.'

Callum came up to the desk as she was speaking. He looked purposeful and energetic, as though he meant business, immaculately dressed in dark trousers, a navy-blue shirt and a subtly patterned grey-blue tie. He was so different from the casually dressed man she'd spent time with on the beach, and yet either way he managed to set her pulse racing.

'Did I hear you talking about Simon Henderson's patient—the three-year-old who thinks it's fun to stick things in his ear?'

Alex nodded.

'I would have had a look at the boy myself,' he said with a frown, 'but I have a patient waiting—I suspect she's had a mini-stroke.' He gave Alex a smile that warmed her through and through. 'You've just come from seeing Dr Langton, I take it? What was it today? Cut back on the use of surgical gloves and paper towels and make do with cheap coffee in the staff lounge?'

She shook her head. 'No, nothing like that. I'm afraid it was much more serious.' She hesitated.

He probably wasn't going to like what she had to say, but she gave him a wry smile and tacked on, 'As far as you're concerned, it means ordering any new equipment is definitely off limits for the foreseeable future.'

His brows drew together. 'I might have guessed. Still, let's look on the bright side—that can't apply to stuff already on order.' He pulled a face. 'I don't suppose there's any news on the transcranial Doppler ultrasound machine I requested, is there?'

Alex sucked in a breath and laid a hand lightly on his arm as though to soften the blow. 'Callum, you know as well as I do that it's not a piece of equipment that would normally be used in the emergency room. You're setting your expectations way too high in this economic climate. You don't have a chance. You know the board won't sanction any undue expenditure.'

Perhaps it was a mistake, touching him. It made her recall all too vividly the way they had sat close together on the beach. A wave of nostalgia hit her. Those few short hours had seemed like stolen moments, and she longed to experience them all over again…but it seemed as though she was wishing on a moonbeam. Her life was complicated enough, without hankering after something that was out of reach. And she and Callum had nothing in common, did they? Their personalities were totally different, and even at work they managed to clash. She let her hand drop to her side.

He laid an arm around her shoulders and looked into her eyes. 'That's as maybe, but refusing to even look at it shows a complete lack of forward thinking on the part of the board.' He grinned. 'I'm pretty sure you could sweet-talk them into changing their minds. With the right diagnostic equipment in place we could save several days of waiting for test results. That way, we could avert imminent strokes, and by taking quick action we could save the hospital money by not having to keep patients in hospital for long periods. You could say it's false economy to avoid having one.'

Alex's mouth made a crooked shape. 'You could say that, and I can see your point, but I'm not at all sure Dr Langton will be convinced by that argument. He's not into long-term solutions right now. All he wants is to see immediate cost-cutting.' She liked having his arm around her. It might not mean anything…it might simply be his way of trying to wheedle her into doing what he wanted, but it still felt good.

'Hmph. So I guess all this means you won't be putting a rush on my order for another bedside X-ray machine, will you?'

She shook her head. 'You already know the answer to that one. No, I won't…not for the fore-seeable future. I did warn you.'

He nodded. 'It's as I thought…but it's a very misguided attitude. The repair bills for the one we're using are getting beyond a joke.' He was thoughtful for a second or two, before adding mischievously, 'And I suppose I'm right in think-ing there's going to be a bit of a wait for my new ECMO machine?'

Alex laughed out loud at that. 'An extracorpo-real membrane oxygenating machine at around a hundred thousand pounds with running costs? I should think so, Callum. That's a very expensive pipe dream.'

His mouth twitched, before turning down at the

corners in mock dismay. 'But one we could do with—after all, we're near the coast, and drowning is just one other way in which a patient might need bypass support for the heart and lungs. Children have been known to recover from drowning in cold water, and with one of those machines on hand to gently warm their blood supply, their chances of survival would be so much greater.'

'I'm with you all the way on that one,' she acknowledged with a smile, 'but it isn't going to happen, I'm afraid. Why don't you get back to the real world and go and save your mini-stroke patient from imminent disaster by giving her the standard treatment?'

'A couple of aspirin, you mean, while I wait for the MRI scanner to be freed up—not likely to be very soon, given the waiting list—or until I can gain access to CT in a few days' time, given that the patient isn't on the critical list?' He made a face. 'A transcranial Doppler ultrasound machine would have given me an accurate diagnosis in a fraction of the time.' He sighed, releasing her, and Alex immediately felt the loss of his comforting arm around her. 'What it is to be working in modern medicine.'

He went on his way and Alex watched his confident stride. How was it that he had found his way into her affections so easily? She had always been careful about the men she let into her life, and yet he seemed to have invited himself, and was completely at ease.

She made an effort to shake off these distracting thoughts, and hurried along to see Dr Henderson's patient in the treatment room.

She could hear the child squealing before she even reached the room, and when she pushed open the door and looked inside, she saw a tearful, red-faced infant rubbing his eyes with his knuckles and glowering at the unfortunate junior doctor. Dr Henderson had relinquished the forceps and was trying unsuccessfully to pacify both the child and his mother. Katie was doing all she could to divert the boy's attention, offering him toys to cuddle and talking to him in a soothing voice, all to no avail.

'Poor Harry,' Alex murmured, going over to

the boy after introducing herself to his mother. 'Is your ear hurting?'

The boy stopped sobbing long enough to nod and stare at her. 'Oh, dear, I'm sorry about that,' she said softly. 'This has all been a bit too much for you, hasn't it? I think we'll give you something to calm you down a bit, and then you'll feel much better.'

She turned to the boy's mother. 'Sometimes these foreign bodies in the ears can slip much further down than we can easily reach and it's obviously troubling him now—but not to worry, I'll give Harry an injection of a sedative and something for the pain, and then we can try again, using suction.'

The woman nodded. 'Thank you. I hate seeing him this way. It's really upsetting.'

'Of course it is. Do you know what it was he put into his ear?'

'A wooden bead. I've told him time and time again not to put things in his ears. He wasn't supposed to play with the beads, but his sister got them out, and he was straight in there. He's into everything these days, like a tornado around the house.'

'It happens a lot, especially with boys,' Alex said in sympathy. She shuddered to think about all the things James got up to… Beth had told her about the time he'd dismantled his toy car and swallowed the button battery. That had meant a swift visit to A and E after it had stuck in his throat.

She prepared the injection and gently explained to the boy what she was about to do. 'Just a scratch,' she said, signalling with a nod of her head to Katie, who was ready to divert him with a toy train.

They waited for the injection to take effect, and when Harry finally appeared to relax and began to take an interest in the toys, Alex showed him the light on the otoscope and explained to him that she was going to use it to look in his ear. 'It's a bit like a torch,' she said.

He seemed happy to go along with that. 'I'll seek out the position of the bead, Simon,' she told the young doctor, 'and then I'll introduce the catheter through the otoscope and apply suction.'

She reached for the catheter that was attached to a wall suction device and after a few fraught seconds carefully located the object that was lodged deep in the child's ear canal. A short time later, she withdrew the catheter along with the bead, which she dropped into a kidney dish. 'There you are,' she told the boy. 'All done.'

Harry's mother smiled, and Simon looked relieved and embarrassed at the same time. 'I hate having to remove these things,' he admitted under his breath. 'It can be such a tricky procedure, and the children are always fractious. You make it look so easy.'

'It just takes practice,' she said lightly, adding with a grin, 'From now on, we'll make sure to give you all the cases that come in when you're on duty.'

Simon looked horrified. 'You don't mean that?'

'Well, maybe one or two...just so you get used to doing it,' she said in a cheerful, placating tone. 'Don't worry...you'll always have help on hand.'

He grimaced, but seemed resigned to his fate, and a few minutes later she left him with the mother and child, and started back towards the main desk.

'Alex…' Katie called her name and fell into step beside her. 'I heard you telling Callum about Dr Langton putting a stop on ordering new equipment. Is that all he's asking for…along with the cost-saving measures you've already put into place?'

Alex shook her head. 'I'm afraid not, Katie. He thinks we should cut staffing levels.'

'By staff, you mean nurses, don't you?' Katie's brow furrowed.

'Yes, but I don't want you to start worrying about that just yet. I'm not planning on making any cuts amongst the general staff. I'll see what I can do by stopping all agency work to begin with. That should make a big difference.'

Katie was still concerned. 'But it will make our jobs harder, too, won't it? How are we to cover for people who are off sick, or cope when we're inundated with patients in A and E? What if we have a major incident to handle?'

'I'm sorry, Katie, I do understand what you're saying, but I'm afraid that's the way it has to be.

We're going through hard times. There just isn't enough money available to cover everything.'

'It's worrying.' Katie frowned.

'Yes, it is. But I promise you I'll do everything I can to keep things running as smoothly as possible. If you have any major problems, let me know and we'll see if we can find a way around things.'

Alex talked to Katie for a little while longer and then went to find her next patient. She worked solidly for the next few hours, and when she had made some headway through the mass of patients on her list, she stopped and stretched her aching limbs and began to think about lunch. Perhaps now that things were a little quieter in the waiting room, it would be a good time to go and grab something to eat. Maybe she could even drop in on Jane for a few minutes, to find out how she was doing.

She left the department, and walked towards the delivery bay close by the open quadrangle where staff sometimes took their lunch. She caught sight of Callum there, talking to a man in uniform while he cheerfully signed a paper attached to a clipboard. She brightened a little. Perhaps they could have lunch together.

She went over to the two men, nodding towards the deliveryman before turning to look directly at Callum. 'Hi,' she said. 'I wondered if we might have lunch together?'

'Ah… there you are,' Callum said quickly, pulling in a sharp breath. He seemed to be distracted by her sudden appearance. 'That sounds like a good idea…though I thought you might already have gone for lunch by now. You're a bit later than usual, aren't you?'

'Yes, I had a heavy workload.'

'Ah.'

She frowned. His manner was definitely a little odd, and she was beginning to wonder why he was so preoccupied. She looked around, wondering what it was that the man in uniform was delivering. Behind him, on a trolley, half-sheltered by the two men, was a huge package, as big as a man and twice as wide. Then it occurred to her that something highly suspicious was going on.

'This looks interesting,' she murmured, peering behind them to glance at the box once more.

'Is this something I should know about? Is this something that's destined for the A and E department?'

'Um...yes,' Callum answered quickly, 'but it's nothing at all for you to worry about.'

'Isn't it?' She lowered her voice, turning away so that the deliveryman wouldn't hear. 'We weren't expecting any deliveries, were we? I thought we'd agreed that any order for new equipment was to go through me first of all?'

'Yes, yes...that's quite true, but everything's in order, so you don't need to worry about it.' He moved her gently to one side, while at the same time saying to the man, 'I'll leave you to take it through to the department, then, Jim. You can leave it where we arranged.'

Jim nodded and Callum turned his attention back to Alex. 'Actually, I'm glad I bumped into you. I was thinking of going up to see Aunt Jane after I've eaten. Do you want to come along? She should be out of the recovery room by now.'

'Yes, of course, I planned to do that, but...' She looked around to see where Jim was taking the package, but the man had disappeared along with his trolley. She frowned. Callum was clearly trying to distract her. 'You're up to something, aren't you?' she said, her gaze thoughtful. 'I specifically said no new portable X-ray machine was to be ordered, and yet somehow you've managed to go behind my back and acquire one.'

'What makes you think it was an X-ray machine?' he said in surprise, raising dark brows. 'All I could see was plain brown packaging.'

'With the words, *Radiology equipment* written in black ink along the base,' she retorted in a laconic tone. 'I suppose you thought you'd sneak it into place while I wasn't looking, and make out it was the one we already have. Did you really think I wouldn't notice the difference?'

He winced. 'Something like that.' He looked her over. 'There's no getting anything past you, is there? You're like a hawk, keeping a beady eye on everything, ready to swoop without warning when you see something you don't approve of.'

'Is that so?' Unaccountably, his description of her stung, and she said crossly, 'Perhaps I wouldn't have to be like that if it wasn't for people like you…haven't you just shown yourself to be a devious, underhanded, sneaky kind of a man who has absolutely no respect for rules and regulations?' Her eyes narrowed on him. 'How could you deliberately flout the new policy that way?'

'I didn't.' He gently placed a hand beneath her elbow and started to lead her towards the quadrangle and the corridor that led to the hospital restaurant.

It was yet more diversion tactics, but she wasn't going to let him wriggle off the hook that easily. 'Didn't it occur to you that I would see the invoice? Or were you hoping to sneak that past me, too?'

He appeared to be giving it some thought. 'I suppose there was always the chance I'd get away with it, for a week or so at any rate. But you must agree with me that the old machine needs a thorough overhaul…it's always breaking down at inopportune moments and then we have to wait for the main X-ray room to be clear for use. And some patients are in too bad a way to be moved, so a bedside X-ray is really convenient…as well as quick and safe.' He looked at her closely, his gaze sweeping over her taut features. 'Surely you understand why I did it?'

She looked at him in frustration. 'Of course I understand, but you know as well as I do that things are tight around here these days and we have to be extra-careful with spending. But you don't seem to care about that. Why else would you spend money we don't have?'

He opened his mouth to answer and she cut him short. 'No, don't answer that. I'll tell you why. You did it because you thought you could get away with it…because that's the kind of man you are, a law unto yourself, totally oblivious to the wider picture, to how your actions will affect everyone else, let alone having any regard for the kind of example you're setting. As long as you get your own way, nothing else matters, does it?'

His dark brows rose. 'Phew!' He whistled softly under his breath and stared at her, his eyes widening. 'I didn't realise you had such a negative opinion of me. Are you quite sure there isn't anything you left out?'

'Oh, I'm sure there's more where that came

from,' she said tersely. 'Give me time, and I'll come up with a list.'

He absently nodded agreement. 'I thought you might...' He studied her. 'I'd no idea I could rouse you so much...you're usually so calm and in control. You never lose your cool. It's what everyone says about you...you don't show what you're thinking. You just get on with the job and deal with everything and everyone efficiently, without any kind of sentiment.'

He studied the quick rise and fall of her chest, his glance roaming over her tense figure, drifting down over the cotton pin-tucked blouse she wore, with its self-coloured buttons, and the slim-fitting skirt that gently skimmed her hips and ended at the knee, to show shapely calves.

'Perhaps things are different now, though,' he murmured. 'Nothing's quite going the way you want it to now that Dr Langton's intervened, and you're having to fight to keep everything in order. You seem quite flushed with the exertion.' Light glimmered in his eyes. 'It makes a very appealing picture, you being all pink and agitated. I'm not at all used to seeing that, though I have to wonder why you're getting yourself so worked up…I might even say passionate…about what you imagine I've been up to.'

'I'm not getting myself worked up.' She ground the words out through her teeth and sent him a stony look. 'I'm just pointing out the error of your ways.'

'Yes, I appreciate that. But I'm still intrigued. This is so unlike you. You never vent your spleen, no matter how provoked you might be.' His expression was quizzical, his glance trailing over the firm jut of her chin and coming to rest on the soft fullness of her mouth. 'I wonder if you'd have reacted the same way if it was any other colleague who had been implicated?' He shook his head. 'Somehow, I doubt it. I have the notion that I'm the only one who can bring out such strong feelings in you.' His eyes glinted. 'Now, there's food for thought.'

She pulled in a shocked breath. 'That's complete nonsense.'

'Is it?'

They went out through the glass doors and into the deserted quadrangle. From here, they would be able to reach the restaurant, which was situated just beyond the dense screen of trees and herbaceous plants.

Alex was deep in thought. He was talking rubbish, wasn't he? Of course she wasn't getting herself all stirred up about him…it was the situation that disturbed her, wasn't it? It couldn't be that he had managed to fire up some spark that lay dormant within her…could it?

She couldn't fathom it out. Why *was* she so het up? Was it really true that he, alone, was able to provoke her to such a wild and deeply emotional response, one that started up in the very core of her being? Surely not? The idea was unthinkable. She sent him a surreptitious glance, at the same time giving an imperceptible shake of her head, as though she was trying to rid herself of the notion, but just at that moment he turned towards her and caught her troubled glance.

'Thinking it over?' he asked, an amused note coming into his voice. 'You're having doubts, aren't you?' He reflected on that. 'Perhaps we should put the theory to the test.'

She looked at him suspiciously. 'What do you mean?'

'I mean, maybe we should find out just how deep your feelings go.' He placed a hand lightly under her elbow, and before she realised what he was doing, he had managed to manoeuvre her into the shelter of a privet hedge. 'Perhaps you're not so cool and unemotional as you make out, and it's all welling up inside you, but you just don't know how to handle those instincts that you've buried deep down.'

She shook her head. 'You're way off beam. Why would I…?' Her voice trailed off in uncertainty as his arms gently slid around her waist.

'Why would you get yourself into a state over me?' he finished for her. He drew her close, so that the softness of her breasts was crushed against the hard wall of his chest and her legs encountered the pressure of his strong thighs. 'Well, let's see now…could it be that you're not quite as immune to normal, human emotions as you think you are?' He lowered his head so that his mouth was just a breath away from hers, and Alex suddenly found that she couldn't think straight any more. She knew that she ought to pull away from him, but although her head told her one thing, her treacherous body was telling her something altogether different. His hands were warm on the gentle slope of her hips and she was discovering that she liked the feeling.

'I don't know what happened to me, why I reacted the way I did,' she said cautiously, trying to keep herself on an even keel. She hesitated, doubts clouding her brain. 'I don't know what came over me.' She frowned, confusion settling on her, so that she was torn between wanting to berate him for his misguided actions, and yet, at the same time, she was conscious of her own shortcomings holding her back and undermining her confidence. And all the while he was holding her, setting her senses on fire with his gently stroking hands and somehow managing to befuddle her wits.

'It's not surprising you feel this way,' he said in a soothing tone. 'You're stressed and overworked. You've taken on far too much...your brother and his wife are seriously ill, you have the children to care for, the house is a work in itself, and on top of all that, you have a difficult job to do. You shouldn't blame yourself. Anyone would bend under the strain.' He ran his hand over the length of her, letting it glide slowly over her back, her hip, her thigh. 'But I can make things easier for you. I can show you how to forget your worries for a while.'

He rested his cheek against hers, his hand lightly caressing her, smoothing over the small of her back, and drawing her into the shelter of his body. 'You just have to let me help you.'

For some reason, she didn't even think of resisting, wanting only to lean into him and take comfort in his nearness…and that was strange, because no man had ever had quite that effect on her before this. Perhaps he sensed that inherent need in her, because after a moment or two he moved even closer, brushing his lips over hers and delicately testing the soft contours of her mouth.

Involuntarily, her lips parted, tantalised by his sweet exploration, and she gave herself up to his kiss, loving the way he moulded her to him and wrapped his arms around her. Somehow, just by holding her and cherishing her this way, he made her feel that she was all woman. For just these few moments she felt utterly feminine and desirable, and she realised that it was a feeling that she had lost over these last few months. She had been so bound up in her work, her problems, that she had forgotten there was more to living than being an automaton. It had taken Callum to bring her to life and show her that she couldn't stay locked up in her ivory castle. Why was it that she let her work and the chaotic demands of family and household chores rule her everyday life?

'Alex?' He lifted his head and looked down at her, reaching up with his hand to smooth away the creases that had formed on her brow. 'You're thinking again. I can feel you thinking... I thought we'd established you should take time out from that?'

'I...I don't know... I didn't realise...' She could feel herself tensing up all over again. 'That's all very well for you to say, isn't it? You seem to sail through life without worrying about anything. I'm the one who has to explain to the bosses when things go wrong. I'm the one who has to come up with answers. I can't just cast it off as though it's nothing.'

He sighed, leaning his head against her forehead. 'This is about the X-ray machine again, isn't it? There's no way you're going to relax until you've resolved it in your mind.'

'You know me so well, don't you?' It was a question tinged with regret. Why couldn't she simply let go, and cast her worries to one side?

'Would it help if I told you that it isn't a new machine?' He frowned. 'It's a reconditioned model—what they euphemistically call "pre-loved". And as to the money to pay for it, I've been raising funds for some time now, through various fun runs and dinner dances, raffles and so on. Now we're reaping the rewards.' He ran his fingers through the silk of her hair. 'So you see, you had no reason to worry. I didn't go against you. In fact, I told you that in the first place.'

'Oh!' She looked at him, aghast. 'And you let me go on…'

'And on…' He chuckled. 'I'd have stopped you, but it occurred to me that you needed to get it off your chest. You've been wound up for days, weeks. All you think about is the job, cost-cutting, and whether or not everyone is toeing the line.'

She stiffened. 'But that's what I'm here for. It's the reason I was set on.'

'But you're not alone in any of this. I'll be there for you. I'm working with you, not against you. I appreciate how difficult the job is for you, and I'll do whatever I can to help you. Together we can sort this out. Believe me.'

She closed her eyes briefly. She wanted to believe him. But in the past those men she had thought she could rely on had always let her down. They didn't want to know about the hassles of the job. All that mattered to them was to take life as it came and if things went wrong, so be it.

She couldn't live like that. She wanted to relax and enjoy life, but she couldn't let it toss her about on a whim, like flotsam and jetsam on a beach. Somehow, if it was in her power, she wanted to make a difference.

Could she trust him? Those few moments of

inner peace, when he had held her in his arms and shown her that another side to life was possible had been so fleeting. Deep down, she recognised that they were two different people, opposites in every way, and yet she was drawn to him, as though by some invisible, magnetic thread.

Now she was more confused than ever.

CHAPTER SIX

'Do you think Mummy will like this?' Sarah asked, adding petals made out of red tissue paper to the flowers that decorated the front of the card she was making. 'It's a vase, see, with lots of flowers in it.'

'I'm sure she'll love it,' Alex said, admiring her efforts. 'It's very pretty, and I know your mother loves flowers.'

'I made a sailboat picture for Daddy,' James put in, waving his card in the air. 'He likes boats. He takes me to sail mine in the brook sometimes.' He frowned, his grey eyes troubled, and Alex wondered if he was thinking about those special times spent with his father, which had come to an abrupt end after the accident.

'You're right, it's perfect for him…and we'll put it on his bedside table at the hospital, so that he can see it as soon as he's feeling a bit better.'

'He's really poorly, isn't he?' Sarah's eyes clouded, and Alex wished there was some way she could comfort her. The children missed their parents and as time went on it was becoming more and more difficult for her to soothe their worries. 'The nurse said he wasn't well enough to see us. She said he had to rest.'

'When are we going to see him again?' James asked. 'I want him to come back home. I want Mummy to come home.'

'I know… It's very difficult for both of you, isn't it?' Alex laid her arms around the children's shoulders as they stood close to one another by the kitchen table. 'But your mother is getting stronger every day, and perhaps it won't be too long before she's able to come home.'

'And Daddy?' Sarah's gaze was almost pleading and it wrenched at Alex's heart not to be able to give her the answer she wanted.

'I don't know. The doctors and nurses are doing what they can to make him more comfortable. We just have to wait, and hope that soon he'll be stronger.'

James's bottom lip trembled, but he didn't say

anything more, and Alex gave him a hug. 'Why don't you finish making your cards for Auntie Jane?' she suggested. 'If you can finish them off in the next few minutes, before I drop you both off at Martha's house, I'll be able to give them to Jane when I go in to work today.'

'She's going to be home soon, isn't she?' Sarah brightened a little. 'You said she had her operation and she was all right.'

Alex nodded. 'She just has to stay in hospital for a couple of days, so the doctors can make sure she's healing up nicely.' Jane's operation had been done with minimally invasive surgery, which meant that the surgeon had made several small incisions and used a laparascope to help with the procedure.

'I don't want to go to Martha's,' James grumbled, his bottom lip jutting. 'I want to stay here with you.'

She knelt down and put her arms around him. 'But I have to go to work, James. You know that, don't you?'

'Yes, but I want you to stay at home. I want you to stay here, with us.'

Alex shook her head. 'I'd like to do that. I wish I could, sweetheart, but it just isn't possible right now. I have to go to work to earn money so that I can pay all the bills. I'd love to stay here with you, but I can't.' Alex frowned. 'Anyway, I thought you liked being with Martha? You have a good time at her house, don't you?'

James didn't answer, but Sarah said quietly, 'She's okay. She takes us to the park—but it's not the same. We like it here with you. The only thing better would be for Mummy and Daddy to come home.'

Alex kissed both of them, wanting to comfort them and reassure them at the same time. 'If I could wave a magic wand and make it happen for you, I would, but for now, we all have to make the best of things.'

She got to her feet and glanced at the table, littered with glue sticks, cards and coloured tissue paper. 'Like I said, if you want me to give the cards to Auntie Jane, you'd better get a move on, because we have to leave here in twenty minutes.'

She arrived at the hospital some time later, feeling harassed and dejected. James had begun to play up as she'd dropped him off at her neighbour's house, and it had taken all her ingenuity and powers of reasoning to soothe him and help him to settle down. It also meant that she was a few minutes late for work, and that added to her stress levels, leaving her flustered.

'We're short-handed,' Katie told her as she made her way to the main desk. 'The waiting room's full and we don't have enough nurses to cope with the workload. Charlotte's off sick, and Simon Henderson is away on a course.' She shook her head. 'I don't know how we're going to manage things.'

'I know it's difficult, but we'll just have to keep going as best we can,' Alex told her, giving it some thought. 'Unfortunately, I can't bring in any locum doctors, and we won't be using the agency nurses any more. It means that your job, triage, is more important than ever, because we'll probably need to allocate nurses to the most serious cases. Waiting times will be stretched, of course, but there's nothing we can do about that in the circumstances.'

Katie sighed. 'We'll do what we can.'

'Thanks, Katie. You're all very good at what you do, and I'm just hoping that you'll be able to keep things together for as long as possible.'

She took a moment to glance at the status board. An infant was coming in by ambulance…something else to turn up her stress levels a notch. Very young, sick children were always a source of concern.

'Did I hear something about waiting times?' Callum came over to the desk. He placed a chart in the tray and picked out another one, just as Alex reached for a file. Their hands brushed against one another, sending small explosions of sensation to rocket through Alex's arm. She sucked in a breath. Why was it that her senses went on overdrive every time he came near? She stole a glance at him, but looked away when his gaze met hers. It didn't help that he always looked so good, either. Her heartbeat had quickened and there was a strange ache starting up inside her. He was way too distracting. He wore dark trousers and a shirt that moulded his body and showed off the flat plane of his stomach, hinting at the vital, energetic man within, a man who was always on the go and kept himself totally fit.

'Waiting times are getting longer,' Katie said. 'It's the budget cuts coming home to roost.' She moved away, heading towards the treatment room.

Callum's brows drew together. 'There's no easy answer, is there?' He glanced at Alex, who was trying to clear her head of errant thoughts by attempting to concentrate on her work schedule and make some sense of it. She was not going to let herself get worked up about him. It was her hormones that were bothering her, nothing else. 'No,' she said. 'The problem is, we need more money, not less.'

She frowned at her work schedule. How was she going to pull in her clinic time as well as take in another meeting with the executive board? Dr Langton seemed to forget that she had other priorities when he called these impromptu gatherings. And in the meantime, would it help to cheer up the nurses if she bought in pizzas and cookies to keep them going through the busy times when they weren't able to get away for a proper break?

It was surely worth a try. She made a mental note to phone the local take-away food shop to arrange delivery.

'You look a little flushed,' Callum said, sending her a thoughtful glance. 'Is it the staffing problem, or something else? I saw you come flying in here a couple of minutes ago as though the hounds of hell were at your feet.'

Alex made a helpless gesture with her hands. He was looking at her so intently and she wanted so desperately to be close to him. She was trying not to think about the way he had kissed her not too long ago, or about the way it had felt to be wrapped in his arms.

'It's the children, mostly,' she murmured, 'James and Sarah. It's very worrying. They're both finding it difficult to cope with their parents in hospital, and I don't know what to tell them now that Ross has taken a turn for the worse. I'm becoming really anxious about him. And now that school has broken up for the holidays they're saying that they want me to be there for them.' She gave a sigh. 'I feel as though I'm being torn all ways.'

'There's no perfect solution to any of those, is there? Given a choice, I suspect children are always going to want their parent or guardian close at hand…but in this day and age even in the best of circumstances I guess it isn't always possible.'

She shook her head. 'No, it isn't. I've been thinking about it, and maybe I'll try to get them enrolled in some play activities over the next few weeks. That might help to distract them a bit.'

'Good idea. That could work out well.'

A siren sounded in the distance, and they both turned towards the ambulance bay. 'This must be the two-year-old we've been expecting—the one with the high temperature and vomiting,' Callum said. 'Would you be able to work with me? I've a feeling we'll need your skills as a paediatrician with this one.'

She nodded, walking briskly alongside him. 'Do we know anything about her condition? The GP sent her to us, didn't he?'

'That's right. Apparently, she had chickenpox a few weeks ago, and since then she's been going rapidly downhill. She's been generally unwell, lethargic and showing signs of irritability. Her mother complains that she's gone off her food over the last few days, and now she's very poorly.'

They hurried to greet the ambulance technicians, who were wheeling the child into the department. 'This is Rachel Vernon,' the paramedic said. 'She's two years old. She had a couple of seizures in the ambulance, so we've given her medication to control them, but her condition's still unstable. There are signs of neck rigidity and photophobia.'

Callum nodded grimly. 'Thanks,' he said, taking over and accompanying the infant into the treatment room. He gently began to examine the child while Alex talked to the girl's parents.

'It's bad, isn't it?' the father said, his face taut with anxiety. 'She looks so ill. The GP said it might be meningitis.'

'It's a possibility,' Alex agreed. 'Meningitis means that the meninges, the brain's protective covering, are inflamed, but I'm concerned that the seizures are a sign that there's inflammation within her brain, too. We'll do tests to find out exactly what's causing her problems, though, and in the meantime we'll give her supportive treatment.'

She tried to reassure the parents that they would do everything possible to help their child. Then she turned to Callum, wanting to know the results of his examination.

'It's possible we're dealing with a viral infection,' he said, 'but if that's the case, it's more serious than usual. This little girl is very sick.' His expression was sad as he looked at the infant, but there was something else in his eyes that Alex had learned to recognise, a growing determination, perhaps, that he would do his utmost to pull the child through this distressing illness and get her back on her feet once more. He straightened. 'I'll get a CT scan done as soon as possible.'

Alex nodded. 'I agree. I'd recommend antibiotics as a cover, until we know what we're dealing with, along with medication to bring her temperature down and control her pain, and something to stop the vomiting. And we need to do a lumbar puncture as soon as she's stable.' A lumbar puncture would show them whether they were dealing with a bacterial or a viral infection, and once they knew the nature of it, they would be able to choose the most appropriate treatment.

He nodded and briefly addressed the nurse who was assisting. 'I'll give the child a corticosteroid to control the inflammation, along with an anti-convulsant, and at the same time we'll set up an EEG so that we can monitor any more seizures. Later on we may need to start an infusion of mannitol to control any rise in intracranial pressure. In the meantime, we'll take blood for testing, and I'm going to ask the lab to get back to us urgently with the results.'

'Okay, I'll organise a trolley.' The nurse hurried away to prepare the equipment.

Some time later, when they had done all they could to safeguard the child and make her more comfortable, Alex and Callum spoke once again to the parents, before finally turning their attention to their other patients.

'We'll look at the possibility of doing a lumbar puncture in a few hours,' Callum said. 'It all depends how well she responds to the initial treatment.'

'Waiting's always difficult,' Alex said, frowning. She could see that he was worried about his small patient, but their options were limited right now. They were doing everything possible to control the infection, but until they knew exactly what they were dealing with, they were working in the dark. 'Given that she's just suffered a bout of chickenpox, it's quite likely that we're dealing with a viral source...the abnormalities on the EEG certainly seem to point that way, but without the lab tests we can't know for sure.'

They both went their separate ways after that, treating a variety of patients who had come in with all manner of problems from fractures to worrying chest infections.

Around lunchtime, Alex met up with Callum again as she was suturing a gash in a child's hand. He put his head around the door of the treatment room, and said quietly, 'Rachel hasn't had any more seizures since we last saw her, so I'm thinking we might do the spinal tap after lunch. Right now, though, I'm going up to see my aunt... I thought you might want to come with me as soon as you're free. I'll be in the staff lounge, grabbing a bite to eat.' He gave her a knowing wink.

'I heard some good fairy had pizza sent in, along with baguettes and cakes and other goodies.'

Her mouth curved. 'Just give me a minute to finish up in here.' She glanced at her young patient a short time later. 'That's it…we're all done, Lewis. The nurse will put a dressing on the hand for you, and then you're free to go home with your mum.' She smiled. 'You've been very brave,' she added, presenting him with a teddy-bear badge and a page to colour, and he left the room with a beaming smile on his face.

She found Callum in the lounge, tucking into a bacon-filled baguette. 'These are good,' he said, munching appreciatively. 'You want to try one?'

She nodded. 'Perhaps I will.' She could see from what was left in the boxes that her gesture had gone down well with the staff. Katie and a couple of the other nurses on their lunch break were tucking in.

'There's a rumour going around,' Katie said, swallowing the last dregs of her tea and rinsing her cup at the sink. 'People are saying that Dr Langton will use the reduction in staff as an excuse to cut down on the emergency department's hours.'

Alex frowned. 'I haven't heard anything like that. When I told him that we were on budget to keep the department up and running, he agreed with me.'

Katie made a face. 'I wonder how much we can trust him. My friend worked at a hospital where he was an executive some time ago. He closed her unit down and transferred the services to the city hospital several miles away.'

Callum was thoughtful for a moment or two. 'I suppose, with the cuts in place, he could say that we don't have the people to man the unit, and therefore we'll no longer be able to provide a twenty-four-hour service.'

Alex's eyes widened. 'That isn't going to happen here. I'm making these changes for the good of the department. I'm not going to stand by and watch the A and E unit be disbanded.'

'Well, I thought it only right to warn you.' Katie made her way to the door. 'But thanks, anyway, for the food. It helps a lot. There's nothing like a full stomach to give people a boost.'

Alex watched her go out into the corridor, followed by the other nurses, leaving them alone in the room. Could there be some truth in what Katie had said? She brooded on the subject for a moment or two before going over to the table and picking out a slice of pizza.

'Try not to worry about it,' Callum said, studying her taut features. 'You're doing the best you can. I don't see how you can do any more.' He gave a crooked smile. 'As it is, you're like a whirlwind at the best of times, coming up with all these ideas for savings, starting new practices and setting up new audits. Since you arrived, no one's really had time to gather breath.'

'Oh.' The word came out on a faintly shocked exhalation. What was she to say to him? 'Is that really how you see me?'

'I think you believe in getting the job done. You don't think about failure…and that's a good thing.'

'Is it?' She nibbled at the pizza. 'Right now, if there's any truth in what Katie says, it looks as though failure's staring me in the face. It seems that whatever I do, Dr Langton will try to close us down.'

'But we won't let that happen, will we?' He smiled at her. 'I've been thinking about what you said—about the hospital needing more money, not less. Perhaps there's a way we can make that happen.'

'Oh?' She was intrigued. 'I'm not sure how we could do that, unless we offered paid services of some sort.' She finished the pizza and wiped her hands on a serviette.

He nodded. 'That's exactly what I was thinking. Maybe we could rent out facilities that aren't being used, if not full-time, then on a part-time basis...like the theatres and the scanner, for instance.'

She thought about it. 'You're right,' she said, her mouth curving. 'And maybe we could rent out some of the outpatient facilities that aren't used at weekends. That way, we could perhaps have a GP-run minor injuries unit to take some of the strain off A and E.'

'See? You're getting the idea.' He came and put his arms around her. 'I told you I would help.'

'And you have, brilliantly.' She tilted her face up to him, glad to have him hold her and keep her close. 'I could put those suggestions to the board. It would make such a difference—it's a whole new way of thinking.'

He ran his hands along her arms. 'So maybe now you'll be able to think less about work, and more about getting some much-needed rest and recuperation along the way. I was thinking of maybe a trip out somewhere…an afternoon in the hills, or a few more hours by the sea, or perhaps we could drive out to Cheddar some time?'

'Oh, what bliss.' She smiled up at him. 'You make it sound so tempting. And I did have such a good time the other day. It was so lovely to walk with you over the rocks and then sit with you and watch the waves break on the shore.'

He dropped a kiss lightly on her mouth, making her whole body tingle with pleasure. 'Then we'll do it again, soon.'

He moved away from her as the door opened and one of the junior doctors came in. Alex drew in a quick breath. How had she let herself be tempted into such a situation at work of all places? All sensible thoughts seemed to go out of her head the moment Callum touched her. Emotionally, she was all over the place at the moment, and it was so unlike her to be this way. What was happening to her?

Perhaps it was simply that she was of an age to be settling down and having children of her own. Up to now, she had bypassed that route, but thinking about it, a distinct pang of loss ran through her.

For an instant, as she tried to imagine how things might be, she could see herself quite clearly with a family of her own, living in the beautiful, sprawling, mellow house with the orchard and acres of land. Subconsciously, hadn't she chosen it because it was a place where she could put down roots?

She thought about it some more. All the children in her surreal vision would not be like her, she was sure of that. They would take after their father, a man who was laid-back, carefree, taking life as it came...the complete opposite of her...

It was odd how these images clamoured to be seen, showing her two sides of a coin, almost as though she was fighting a battle within herself, and she tried to shake off the strange feelings that were assailing her. What was wrong with her? Perhaps she'd been overdoing things. That had to be the explanation.

Callum cut in on her thoughts. 'Perhaps we should go and see Jane while we have the chance?' he suggested.

She nodded, draining the last dregs of her coffee. 'She should be feeling a bit better by now, I expect.'

'Let's hope so. It's been twenty-four hours since the tumour was removed, and by all accounts the surgery went well. Her blood pressure is settling down nicely, too, according to the nurse on duty.'

'It all sounds positive, at any rate.' They left the lounge together and made their way up to the ward.

'It's good to see both of you,' Jane said with a smile as they entered the room. It was a small bay, with four beds, and she was sitting in a chair by the window, looking out over the hospital grounds. For the moment, she was the only oc-cupant. 'The others have gone to the day room,' she told them, 'except for one lady, who's having physio.'

She caught her breath as she spoke, as though she was in pain, and began to rub absently at her side. Alex frowned. 'Are you all right? How are you feeling?'

'I'm okay,' Jane answered. 'A bit bruised, I think. It's gone a bit purple-looking around here.' She waved a hand vaguely over her upper abdomen. 'It hurts when I breathe, but that's probably only to be expected after the surgery.'

Callum was instantly alarmed. 'May I see? Has the doctor been to look at you since the operation?'

'Yes, dear.' She patted his hand, and allowed him to check the bruising. 'I went to have an ultrasound scan this morning...' She paused to gather her breath. 'I think they were just checking everything's all right. They didn't say much to me about it. The technician said she has to send the results to the doctor, and I'll be seeing him again, later today, apparently.'

Callum stood up, tension evident in his whole body, and Alex understood his reaction perfectly.

The purple bruised area was not what they should have expected to see. 'Why wasn't I told about this?' he asked, almost as though he was talking to himself.

'I'm telling you now,' Jane said.

'But the medical staff should have kept me informed.' He shook his head, frowning. 'I must go and find out about this. I need to know what's going on. Excuse me. I'll be back in a little while.'

He left the room and Jane sighed. 'Oh, dear. Now there's going to be trouble.'

'I'm sure he'll be very thoughtful in how he goes about things.' Alex gave her a reassuring smile, keeping her own anxieties about Jane's condition to herself. Jane was looking worried, and perhaps the best thing she could do was wait until Callum returned with details of what was actually wrong before she made any comment.

'He loves you dearly, you know,' she said. 'He won't rest until he knows you're up and about and feeling strong again.' She gave her the get-well-soon cards the children had made for her. 'And you've made a lasting impression on James and Sarah, too.'

'Bless them. These are lovely.' Jane looked at the cards, Sarah's bright with a basket full of paper flowers, and James's a mouth-watering design of a delicious-looking cherry cake.

'James is looking forward to you being home and filling the house with the smell of baking,' Alex told her. 'He says it's the best thing in the world. Of course, to be fair to him, his instincts aren't entirely selfish. He's really fond of you... but he just loves your cooking, too.'

'Oh, he's a treasure.' Jane chuckled. 'He does so remind me of Callum when he was a youngster. He was always up to something, and he could wind me around his little finger when he wanted.' She paused to rest for a while, lightly rubbing at the ache in her side. Then she glanced at Alex and said, 'So, how are things with you? Are you managing with the children? I know it must be difficult for you, especially with your brother taking a turn for the worse.'

'We're coping,' Alex said. 'Martha's been a great help. I'm really glad you put us in touch with each other.'

'Well, I knew you would need some help.' Jane

was quiet for a moment, studying her features. 'Something's wrong, though, isn't it? I could tell as soon as you walked in. You're not yourself. Is it the job? Or Callum? Have you two been fighting?'

'Me…fight with Callum?' Alex gave a self-conscious laugh. 'Heaven forbid! I'd never win… I thought I was strong-minded and on the ball, but he runs rings around me without even trying.'

Jane was very perceptive. Nothing much escaped her, did it? Even when she was ill. 'I think he feels I'm a workaholic.' She gave a faint sigh. 'I don't see how I can do things differently. I was given a job to do, and I'm getting on with it as best I can.'

'Ah, well, you shouldn't mind him too much. Most likely, he's speaking from personal experience there. His feelings go way back to his childhood, and it was always a bone of contention for him that his mother was so often away from home. Of course, she had an important job to do. He always understood that, and she always tried to make up for it once she was back with him. I dare say he has mixed feelings about the whole business of career women. I think that's why he's never settled down. I have the feeling he was put off by his parents' way of life—he saw how the idea of parents and family could go wrong and he doesn't want to risk that for himself.'

Alex frowned. He'd told her once, some time ago, that he preferred to be footloose and fancy-free, and she'd taken it to mean that it was just a temporary state of mind. But perhaps the hospital grapevine had it right after all…he was afraid of commitment.

Callum pushed open the door just then and came to join them. He was still frowning. 'I just had a word with the doctor,' he said, going over to his aunt and sitting down beside her. 'It's nothing to worry about, but the reason you're feeling so uncomfortable is that during the keyhole surgery the space for manoeuvre was limited, and it seems that one of the instruments caused a blood clot to form on your liver. It's building up slowly, and that's why you're feeling so uncomfortable.' He glanced at her to make sure that she understood what he was saying.

Jane was puzzled. 'Are they going to do something about it? Or will it go away on its own?'

'The surgeon's going to drain it for you this afternoon, in an hour or so. He's going to come and talk to you about it in a while. It's not a difficult procedure, and he'll do it with the aid of the ultrasound monitor to guide him. He'll anaesthetise the area and give you a sedative, so you won't feel anything, and afterwards you'll be much more comfortable.'

'Oh, I see.' Jane fell silent after that, but there was tension in her shoulders, and Callum gave her a gentle hug. 'I'll stay with you throughout the procedure, if you like. I'll be there to make sure everything's all right.'

'Are you sure you'll be able to do that? Won't you be too busy with your work in A and E?'

'You're more important to me than my work,' he said simply, putting his arm around her. 'If it will make you feel better, then I want to be with you.'

She nodded, and relaxed a little, some of the stiffness leaving her shoulders, and Alex guessed she was more worried than she appeared. She wanted Callum to be with her. He was a comfort to her, and she thought the world of him, as though he was the son she never had. Watching them, Alex almost envied them their closeness. He thought the world of his aunt, and Alex could see that it was a bond that would never be severed.

They stayed and talked to her for a little while longer, and then Callum said reluctantly, 'We have to go back down to A and E to look in on a little girl, but I'll be back with you before you know it. Don't worry about anything.'

'I won't.' She clasped his hand as he lightly kissed her cheek, and then she waved them to the door. 'Go and see to your work,' she said. 'I'll be fine.'

Callum didn't say anything as he and Alex went down to the emergency department. Alex wanted to talk to him, she even opened her mouth to ask him how he was feeling, but he shook his head, cutting her off. His features were shuttered, as though he was working something out within himself, and she just had to accept that this was the wrong time, that she would be intruding if she pushed him to speak.

Just a few minutes later, they worked together to prepare the little girl for the lumbar puncture. She was still very poorly, and Alex was anxious to see that they made the procedure as painless and unobtrusive as possible for her.

'We'll give her a sedative first,' Alex told the nurse, 'and it would be better for her if her mother could come and be with her.'

The nurse nodded. 'I'll make sure we have some toys on hand in case we need to distract her.'

As soon as everything was in place, Callum injected the girl with anaesthetic around the area where they were to do the spinal tap. He waited for it to take effect, and then inserted a needle to withdraw some of the spinal fluid.

Alex labelled the vials and gave them to the nurse to take to the lab. 'We need the results urgently,' she told her.

Once they had finished, they made sure that Rachel was sedated enough so that she would lie still for the next hour or so. Callum checked her medication and made certain that everything was in order, before finally checking his watch.

'I should go,' he said, glancing at Alex. 'Would you take over for me while I'm away?'

'Of course,' Alex said quietly as they left the treatment room. 'You're worried about your aunt, aren't you?' She frowned. 'It's not a difficult procedure, to remove the haematoma, you know. I'm sure she'll be all right.'

He nodded. 'I'm not really concerned about that side of things.' His expression was bleak, his mouth flattening a little as they walked along the corridor. 'It's just that she has always been so strong in every way. Up to now, she's always been there for me whenever I needed her, she would look after me and comfort me when I was ill as a child, and now that the positions are reversed it hurts to see her looking so frail.'

His eyes darkened. 'She won't give any sign that she's worried or upset, but I know that deep down she's afraid and uncertain. And who can blame her? To think that these last few years she's been suffering all these symptoms of high blood pressure and I did nothing about it. I let the doctor go on treating her with tablets that were doing no good whatsoever. I should have spotted that something was wrong sooner and arranged for her to have tests.'

Alex laid her hand on his, causing him to come to a stop by the lift bay. 'As things turned out, you couldn't have done any more than you did,' she murmured, running her fingers along his arm in a gentle caress. 'It was normal procedure to treat her with medication in the first instance, and none of the tests would have shown the presence of a tumour until this late stage. Her condition is really very rare. You can't blame yourself.'

He wasn't convinced. 'You're very sweet, Alex,' he said softly, lifting a hand to gently cup her face. His fingers traced the line of her cheekbone and slid along the angle of her jaw. 'Thank you for trying to make me feel better…but I'm okay, you know. I can handle it. I just have to make sure that she knows I'll be there for her, come what may.'

The lift doors swung open, and they parted company as Callum headed back up to his aunt's ward. Alex turned away to go and seek out her next patient. She could still feel the light touch of his fingers on her cheek, and somehow that made her incredibly sad, and at first she didn't know the reason for that. Perhaps it was because it made her yearn for what she could not have.

Because there was no way she could allow herself to fall for Callum, was there? So far, he hadn't shown that he was the kind of man who was ready to settle down, and for her part, there was far too much going on in her life right now for her to even think of getting involved.

Why, then, was the temptation so irresistible? Right now was the worst possible time for her to be even thinking of starting a relationship, especially one with a colleague…and yet there was no getting away from the fact that she was filled with a longing that couldn't possibly be assuaged.

CHAPTER SEVEN

'IT'S good to see you finally taking time out to relax,' Callum said, sitting down on one of the comfortable patio chairs that Alex had set out on the raised wooden decking just beyond the back of the house. It stood amongst landscaped gardens, with rustic arbours and pergolas that were covered with rambling roses.

'I don't recall you giving me much choice,' Alex said grumpily. The sun was shining down on them from a clear blue sky and she was over-heated and becoming conscious that she would have done better to wear a cotton skirt with her loose, sleeveless top, rather than her jeans. 'One minute I was repairing the boundary fence, and the next you'd taken over and sent me to make cold drinks.' She was still hot with indignation at being moved bodily out of the way and relegated to the kitchen. She had one day off this weekend to get things done, and he had come along and thwarted her plans.

'You have to admit, though, you weren't getting on too well, were you?' Callum gave her an amused look. 'If I hadn't stopped by to pick up some fresh clothes for Aunt Jane, you'd still be struggling with it now. Anyway, before that you were busy in the kitchen making goodies to take into hospital for her—that was very thoughtful of you, so I figured the least I could do was to help you out.'

He'd already helped her out a good deal over the last few days, coming along to fix the tiles on the roof and lend a hand with the painting. 'Well, I felt it was the right thing to do. She was looking so much better yesterday, so I thought she'd be in a mood to appreciate some cookies. And the children enjoyed helping to make them.' She could hear their voices now, coming from the orchard as they played amongst the trees that were burgeoning with fruit.

He nodded. 'I was worried about her, but everything went well, and it's beginning to look as though she'll make a full recovery. And the tumour was benign, so that was the best news of all.'

'Oh, it was such a relief to hear that. Now all she has to do is rest for a couple of days and then with any luck she'll be able to come home.'

'Let's hope so.' He looked at her, his mouth making a crooked line. 'That might work for you, too,' he said. 'You've been looking quite stressed lately, and I can't help feeling that you could do with some days off.'

'Well, don't hope for too much, because it isn't likely to happen.' She shook her head. They both knew they were miles apart when it came to the demands of her job. 'Though I suppose in the end I *am* glad you came along and stopped me today,' she admitted with a rueful smile. 'That fence has been bothering me for ages, and I was struggling a bit with the wood, where it had rotted.'

'Well, there are new planks in position now, so everything's secure and looking good once more.' He gazed around at the colourful, flower-filled garden and then looked beyond it to the meadow that bordered the apple orchard.

'You certainly picked a gem when you bought

this place,' he said on a thoughtful note. 'And all your hard work is paying off at last. You've tidied everything up, the garden, the orchard…and after a lick of fresh paint the house looks like a beautiful, rambling old cottage. It's like something on a picture postcard, with the wisteria round the door and the natural stone wall with the plants growing in the crevices.' He frowned. 'And yet I bet you hardly have time to sit back and enjoy it.'

Alex was wistful. 'I certainly haven't until now. When I took it on, I wasn't at all sure I was doing the right thing—it was rundown and I knew it would be difficult to sort out, but I couldn't help myself—something told me it had potential.' She nodded towards him. 'You're right, it has been hard work, but with your help, we're gradually restoring it to its original state. Things are beginning to come together now really well.'

'I've been surprised how much I've enjoyed helping out.' He smiled. 'I think house renovation could become a new hobby for me.'

'You're certainly good at it. The old inglenook fireplace in the lounge looks great after being spruced up. I hadn't realised the house held so many treasures.'

She lifted the jug from the centre of the table and started to pour out glasses of chilled Sangria. Ice cubes clinked and mingled with slices of melon, apple, orange and lemon. She handed him a glass.

'Thanks.' He took a sip of the bright red liquid, and savoured the taste on his tongue for the moment. 'This is good,' he said, shooting her a quick glance. 'Is there some subtle ingredient I don't know about?'

'That depends on how you usually make it,' she answered. 'I put in red wine, orange juice and ginger ale, and then topped it up with fruit. I added a few cinnamon sticks, too.'

'It's delicious.' He peered at the slices of apple. 'It won't be too long before you're harvesting your own apples,' he mused. 'Have you thought about what you'll do with them? From the looks of things there are going to be masses.'

She shook her head. 'Apart from eating the dessert apples and making pies with the rest? No, I haven't. Though I suppose I could look into the whole business of cider making. At one time it was made here, on the premises, apparently, in all those old outbuildings.'

He smiled. 'And that will mean even more work for you. You're a glutton for punishment, aren't you? I suppose you wouldn't even consider the easy option, selling them to the local shops, would you?'

'I don't know.' She shrugged. 'Maybe. Though the idea of cider making is sort of intriguing— and it's what Somerset's all about, isn't it? So if I did decide to have a go at making my own, I would be part of it, wouldn't I?'

She leaned back in her chair, studying him through her lashes. He was probably right in what he was saying. It was in her nature to take on too much. As it was, she had been working franti- cally from early that morning, trying to catch up with her chores, baking and then tackling some of the repairs to the property, and it had taken Callum's determined efforts to make her stop. That had annoyed her. She had a limited time scale, and she'd been so intent on getting every- thing done, on ticking all the boxes and making

sure things were in order, that when he had intervened she had put up a strenuous fight, only
to lose out.

She was fast discovering that in his casual, un-
concerned way he was every bit as strong-willed
as she was. He was her opposing force, the com-
mon-sense counterpart to her frenetic power hub.

And yet, for all that, in the end, she was thankful for these few moments of peace and tranquil-
lity that he'd given her. For all her misgivings, she
felt better for sitting here, letting the sun warm
her bare arms, and she had him to thank for that.

She liked the fact that he was close by, too,
sitting back in his chair appearing calm and perfectly relaxed. And he was as heart-stoppingly
good-looking as ever. He was dressed in casual
clothes, stone-coloured chinos and a dark cotton
shirt that emphasised his broad shoulders and
brought out the intense blue of his eyes…eyes
that were looking at her now and making her go
hot all over. It was strange how just with a look
he could make her heart quicken and cause the
blood to surge through her veins like wildfire.

The sound of children's voices cut in on her

reverie. 'We want to pick flowers for Mummy and Auntie Jane,' Sarah shouted up to her from the garden. 'Can we cut the sweet peas down by the fence?'

Alex stood up and went over to the deck rail. 'That's okay,' she said. 'Just make sure James is careful with the scissors.'

'I will.' Sarah's fair curls quivered with excitement. 'We want to decorate some flower baskets. Can we use the ones out of the greenhouse?'

'Yes, that will be fine. I'll help you with them later.' She'd have to, otherwise the sweet peas would probably end up bedraggled, with broken stems and crushed petals, and the flower basket displays would be haphazard and lopsided.

Callum came to join her by the rail. 'Flower baskets?' he queried. 'They won't be content with anything so simple as a bunch of flowers, then?'

She smiled. 'You don't know these children, do you? They don't do anything by halves. Next thing, I'll be sorting out flower-arranging plastic foam and helping them create something special in a wicker basket. They're always coming up with ideas for something or other.'

He laughed. 'They obviously take after you. Perhaps it runs in the family. Is your brother as doggedly determined and resourceful as you?'

A shadow touched her features. 'He was,' she said quietly, 'until he had the accident.' She shook her head. 'I just don't know how he's going to come through it. I don't know what to say to the children any more. I try to shield them from what's happening, but all the time I'm afraid for the worst.'

He put his arm around her. 'I'm sorry. That was thoughtless of me. You must be sick with worry.'

'I'm okay.' Her tone was flat. 'I'm just trying to take things one day at a time.'

'I suppose that's all you can do for now.' He held her close, letting his head rest against hers. 'You amaze me, Alex, the way you get on and cope with life. You don't let anything faze you for too long, do you? You have this marvellous ability to forge ahead and get through things, no matter what.'

She gave a faint smile. 'Some people simply say I'm stubborn and don't listen to reason, but that I keep on going regardless.'

He shook his head. 'I don't see it that way. I have nothing but respect for the way you deal with everything that comes along. Given what you've had to cope with, I suspect a good many women would have given up by now and settled for the easy life…a rented property, an undemanding job, keep the children quiet with videos and a selection of DVDs…but you've done the opposite. You've grabbed life head on and given it a good shake. I think that's remarkable.'

'I'm glad you think so,' she murmured. 'I just wish I felt as strong as you imagine I am. For myself, most of the time, I feel bewildered, lost, under pressure, a little scared about what's to happen.'

He drew her into his arms and held her close. 'You don't have to feel that way,' he said softly. 'I'm here for you. Remember that. I'll do whatever I can for you.'

She lifted her face to him. He looked as though he meant it, as though his words were heartfelt, and it warmed her to think that he would want to be by her side in this, to help her through it. It was comforting to feel that she could rely on him to take some of the burden from her. 'Thank you,' she whispered. 'That means a lot to me.'

His head lowered a fraction, until his lips gently brushed hers, and in the next moment he was kissing her, slowly, with infinite care, as though she was the most precious thing in all the world. Alex gave herself up to that kiss, revelling in the feel of his long body next to hers, loving the way his hands moved over her and lightly shaped her body.

This was more than just a kiss. It was an expression of tenderness, of warmth, of wanting to take care of her, and yet, soon, it became much more than that. There was a growing passion, a sudden heated desire that started as a flicker and developed into an all-consuming blaze.

He deepened the kiss and his body moved to pressure hers, almost as though he would meld with her and claim possession. His breathing became ragged, and Alex clung to him, wanting more, overcome by the frenzied outpouring of sensuality that had overtaken both of them.

'I want you so much, Alex,' he said in a roughened voice. 'You drive me wild with wanting you. Somehow, when I'm with you like this, it's all I can do to hold back. You've put some kind of spell on me. I don't know what it is that you do to me to make me feel this way.'

She cupped his face with her hands, and then slid them down over the hard wall of his chest. She felt the same way. She wanted him, and it was an overpowering feeling, something that she'd never felt before with such intensity.

'This is madness,' she murmured huskily, her breathing coming in quick, short bursts. 'We're worlds apart, you and I.' But it was a madness that devoured her all the same, one that took over her soul. She returned his kisses with feverish abandon, running her hands over his arms, his shoulders, wanting more than this, needing him to show her that he cared enough to be there for her for ever. She was stunned by the intensity of her feelings. She had never before felt this way about any man.

It was an earth-shattering moment of realisation for her. Because, for all their differences, and despite all her guarded emotions, she realised she was falling for him. How had it happened? She was filled with doubts. Was it simply an over-whelming desire that had crept up on her out of the blue? She didn't know. She couldn't tell. She had never experienced anything like it before.

'Auntie Alex, come and see how many flowers we've collected.'

James's childish voice registered on Alex's con-sciousness like a bolt of electricity. It startled her and pulled her back into the reality of where she was and what was going on. She stared up at Callum and laid her fingers shakily against his chest.

'I have to talk to them,' she said in an unsteady voice. 'I have to see to the children.'

She eased herself away from him, and he let her go, reluctantly, watching her as she turned to look over the deck rail once more. 'You've been very busy, haven't you?' she managed, trying to keep her voice even. James's grey eyes were bright with enthusiasm, and Sarah was bursting with energy and eager to get on. The children had filled both baskets with the delicate flow-ers, more than enough to make a couple of gift presentations. 'Take them into the house and put the stems in some cold water in the sink. I'll be there in a minute or two.'

James nodded gleefully and ran off towards the house, leaving Sarah to follow.

'Are you all right?' Callum wound his arms around her once more and looked at her cautiously.

'I don't know,' she said. It was one thing for her to be taken up with the heat of the moment and to have given way to her emotions, but what was really going on inside his head? How did he actually feel about her? 'I feel a bit strange to be honest. I'm not sure I understand what just happened... I think I need to get my head straight.'

He smiled ruefully. 'That goes both ways, I guess. I can't say I was expecting to feel the way I do. Perhaps it's the midafternoon sun that's getting to both of us.'

She frowned, trying to gather her thoughts together. Was he regretting what he'd said just a few moments ago and trying to find a way out? Perhaps it was just as well that they'd been interrupted.

'Maybe.' She looked at him, her gaze troubled.

'I should go and see what the children are up to,' she said.

He nodded acknowledgement of that, and slowly released her. 'I know.'

She added hesitantly, 'Do you want to stay and have some tea with us?' She wasn't altogether sure how she would cope, having him close by for the rest of the afternoon. She was already overwhelmed and confused.

He shook his head. 'I think I'd better go,' he said with some reluctance. 'I promised I would take some clean nightwear into hospital for my aunt, along with a few bits and pieces she asked for, magazines and so on.'

'Okay. You could take the cookies in to her, if you like.'

'Will do.'

She saw him off a few minutes later, feeling sad to see him go, as though she was losing something special. Then she went back into the house and tried to push those thoughts aside and give all her attention to the children. She spent the rest of the afternoon making flower baskets with them.

With any luck, they would stay fresh until they could take them along to the hospital.

'Can we go and see Mummy tomorrow?' Sarah asked. 'I want to see if she can come home soon.'

Alex nodded. 'I have to work, but Martha said she would take you there. She wants to go and see Auntie Jane.'

Alex's weekend break came to an end all too soon, and she was left feeling frustrated at not having achieved all she wanted, as well as being slightly out of synch. There were never enough hours in the day to do everything that was necessary, and it left her irritable and out of sorts. Perhaps the workload was beginning to get to her.

Worrying about her brother didn't help the situation. She pulled in her visits to Ross, Beth and Jane first thing next morning, before she started work, and that only added to her anxieties. Ross was in a bad way. He was breathless, breathing fast and he was complaining of chest pain.

'We're going to get an X-ray of his chest,' the nurse on duty told her. 'And, depending what that shows, the doctor might order a CT scan. There was a lot of trauma to his chest, initially, but after surgery we thought he was on the mend. This is a complication he could do without.'

Alex nodded. 'Will you let me know what happens? I'll be down in A and E, but you can page me at any time or use my mobile number.'

'I will.'

Things were no more settled down in the emergency unit. In fact, when Alex walked towards the department a few minutes later, she found her way to the main doors was blocked by a throng of news reporters, all shouting questions towards a small group of doctors and nurses.

'So how do you feel about the threatened closures?' one man asked. He thrust his recording device towards Katie, who was obviously the spokeswoman for the nurses.

'I believe it will do irreparable harm to patients,' Katie told him. 'They will be diverted to the new hospital some fifteen miles away, and that means treatment will be delayed for precious minutes. People who live locally are being denied the services they need.'

The reporter turned to the others and began

asking more questions. 'Why is the board considering making this move?'

'It's all about budget cuts,' Simon Henderson answered. 'The hospital is running out of money.'

Alex worked her way to the fringes of the group. 'What's going on here?' she said urgently, keeping her voice low as she drew Katie to one side.

'Oh, you won't have heard, will you? You weren't here.' Katie frowned. 'Dr Langton's threatening to close the A and E department down at night. He laid the plans out in a circular he distributed to the staff late yesterday. He thinks we can save money by staying open for fewer hours, but it makes us think that will just be the beginning.'

'Is it actually going to happen, or is it just a threat?' Alex was bewildered by the news. 'Why have the press been called in? How did they get to hear about it?'

'As soon as we read the circular, we thought they should be kept informed. Maybe if the public know that their emergency department could be lost to them, they'll be able to influence the hospital board and persuade them to drop their plans. That's what Callum believes, anyway. He thought our idea of bringing in the press was a good one.'

'Callum? He's part of this?'

'Very much so.' Katie nodded. 'He's over there, speaking to a journalist from one of the nationals.'

Alex pulled in a sharp breath. 'I'll go and talk to him.'

Involving the press was a bad move, bad for everyone. It meant that people would be tense and antagonistic and much less likely to listen to reason, and it would probably irritate the members of the board and cause them to react in a negative fashion. This whole thing was wrong.

She turned to look back at the reporters as Callum's voice suddenly sounded loud and clear. 'If Oakdale's services are moved to the new city hospital, lives could be put in danger. We have to fight this. Asthmatics, patients with heart conditions or kidney disease—all these could suffer if they have to travel long distances for emergency treatment. This is a bad policy. It will be a bad day for the people who live locally if this plan is allowed to go ahead.'

Alex's expression was bleak as she watched him. He had the attention of everyone present. They were hanging on his every word, eager to capture his thoughts and take the story back to their newsrooms. How could he do such a thing without talking to her first? He knew how hard she'd worked to keep the unit viable by making savings, and he knew how much it meant to her to succeed.

She moved towards him, only to be waylaid by one of the reporters who read her name badge and thrust his tape recorder towards her. 'You're one of the managers here, Dr Draycott? What do you have to say about the proposed closure?'

She took a deep breath. 'I'd say that's all it is...a proposed measure. Nothing has been decided, and there are other options still to be considered. We've already made substantial changes to ensure the smooth running of the emergency department, whilst still being able to work within a limited budget—but there are other steps we can take. It's my opinion that services should continue to be provided here at Oakdale, and I shall be talking to the members of the board with suggestions as to how we can do that.'

The reporters threw a barrage of questions at her, but she stepped back, saying briefly, 'Excuse me, please. I have to go to work. As soon as there are any detailed announcements, please be assured you'll be the first to hear them.'

She pushed through the main doors and went into the A and E department. She pulled in a deep breath. How could she have been pushed into defending her ground like that? How could Callum have let it happen?

'You stood your corner well, back there,' he said, coming up alongside her a minute or so later. 'It must have come as a shock to you, to walk into that.'

'It certainly did.' She sent him a troubled glance. 'Why on earth would you want the press involved? And how do you imagine I feel, when you know how hard I've worked to keep things running smoothly? It's as though you've pulled the rug out from under my feet. You know Dr Langton can't make a move without the approval of the board—this was all unnecessary. I'd ex-pected more from you. I'd hoped you would sup-port me.'

'I do support you, and if you'd been here yes-terday I would have brought you in on what we were planning—but, believe me, Dr Langton would have gone to the press sooner or later. As soon as we saw the circular, we realised he'd reverted to his old style. It's what he did when he worked at the other hospital, and we felt we had to gain the upper hand, one way or another. The new hospital building in the city is his pet project. It's beginning to look as though he has no loyalty to Oakdale. He thinks services should be centralised and that's what he's pushing for.'

'But Dr Langton doesn't have the final say in this.' She frowned. 'He's just one member of the board, and if the rest of them disagree he'll have to go along with the majority decision. You're all assuming it's a done deal. It isn't, and I'm just so disappointed that you could throw away everything I've done as if it was of no account, and that you have so little faith in me.'

'Alex, you're putting the wrong interpretation

on this. It isn't that we don't appreciate what you've done. You've done your very best in a difficult situation. But going on past history, Langton is a law unto himself. He's totally single-minded, and once he's decided on something, he's not easily diverted.'

'We'll have to see about that, won't we? All I know is that you kept me out of the loop and went ahead without talking to me. I feel so let down.' She started to move away from him, her shoulders stiff, her whole body tense.

'This isn't about you, Alex, or the way you've done your job.' He caught up with her and laid his hands on her shoulders, his grasp warm and firm. 'It's about Dr Langton and his policies. You're overreacting.'

She was stunned by his comment. 'You think I'm overreacting?' She shook her head. 'How exactly would you expect me to react? You're handing Dr Langton a publicity coup—how do you think he's going to respond to this? He'll bring out all the arguments for placing the new foundation hospital at the centre of things. Oak-dale will become yesterday's news. Well, let me tell you—that's not going to happen if I have anything to do with it.'

'Alex, you need to listen—'

'No, I don't think so.' She started to walk briskly away from him, and didn't stop when he called after her. She was going straight up to Dr Langton's office to deal with this matter at its heart.

'I'm sorry, but Dr Langton is not seeing anyone at the moment,' his secretary told her when she walked into his office a short time later.

'I believe he'll see me.' Alex walked across the room and knocked on the inner door. Then she opened it and went in.

'Alex…' Dr Langton was startled.

His secretary followed Alex into the room. 'I'm sorry Dr Langton…' She hesitated, appearing flustered. 'I told her that you were busy and not free to see people this morning.'

'It's all right, Natalie.' He waved her away. 'You can leave us alone…just hold my calls for a few minutes, will you?'

Natalie withdrew, shutting the door behind her, and Dr Langton sent Alex a cautious look. 'You seem upset, my dear,' he said. 'Is there something I can do for you?'

'Yes, I'm upset.' Her glance ran over him. 'And, yes, there is something you can do for me. Perhaps you can explain to me why you've circulated plans to close down the A and E department without even consulting with me first of all. Wouldn't it have been a professional courtesy to keep me informed of what you had in mind? And perhaps you can tell me why are you even considering closure when there are so many alternatives available to us?'

'Ah…so you've heard about that?'

'Oh, yes. There's a gaggle of press outside the main doors, all clamouring for information, and I was caught up in it without having any warning or knowledge of what it was all about.'

'The press?'

'The press,' she confirmed. 'Did you not expect word to get out?'

'Well, maybe not so soon…'

'The thing is, Dr Langton, I feel you should have kept me informed of your plans regarding A and E. You put me in a difficult position, having to defend management strategies. As I understand it, you think we can cut down on the hours that the department is open and gradually divert services elsewhere. Am I right in thinking that way?'

She waited for him to answer.

He cleared his throat. 'Ahem… It does seem to me that the community might be better served if services were more centralised. I felt that by putting out a circular we might put forward the ideas for change and at the same time gauge the reaction of the staff.'

'But you didn't consult with me first. I'm saddened that you didn't feel able to share your ideas with me—it might have saved a lot of distress if you'd done that—because unfortunately your circular has upset a lot of people.'

'I would have included you, of course, my dear, but the timing seemed right, with the board meeting coming up shortly. It was all a bit rushed, I have to confess, but I think the board members will most likely agree with my proposals.'

'Yes, it was rushed. And as you've said, the whole matter still has to go before the board. I have to disagree with your notion about the out-come. I don't believe the closure of the A and E department, at night or permanently, is a fore-gone conclusion at all. And I do feel that there are still so many proposals to lay before them so that they will think twice about any reduction in the A and E services.'

He spread his hands in an open gesture. 'Of course, you're entitled to your opinion. I know you've worked tremendously hard, but we have to think of these things on a larger scale. We have to think what would best serve the wider community.'

Alex's mouth firmed. 'We also have to think of the local community. Oakdale has a great reputa-tion for being one of the best hospitals around, and its A and E unit is second to none. I won't see it obliterated in order to justify the expense of a foundation hospital. A good many people who live around here owe their lives to this emergency department, as do the tourists who come to the area every summer. Believe me, Dr Langton, I won't stand by and see it fall by the wayside.'

She left his office in a flurry of determination.

After all the meetings she'd had with him, all the different ways she'd come up with to pare down expenses, he'd turned his back on her and gone his own way. Well, he would regret that. The board would hear of her ideas for boosting the hospital budget and there would be no more going through Dr Langton first—he hadn't been considerate enough to consult with her. Instead, she'd email her suggestions to them and follow them up at the next board meeting. She was on good terms with the other executive members and she would see what they had to say about all this.

She was still disturbed by the whole business when she went back to her office in A and E. She sat down at her desk and rattled off a round-robin email, pressing the 'send' button just as Callum knocked on her door and walked in.

'Is it safe for me to come in or are you likely to throw things at me?' he asked, making a show of protecting himself with his hands.

'I don't find any of this the least bit funny,' she said in a dry tone.

'No, actually, neither do I.' He glanced at the

computer monitor. 'I should say, though, it might not be wise to send off emails while you're upset.'

'Are you saying you don't trust my judgement?'

'I didn't say that.' He came and perched on the edge of her desk and she shot him a cool glance. 'I'm just warning you, that's all,' he murmured, 'in case you might do something you come to regret.'

'I don't regret any of my actions. Perhaps Dr Langton will think things through, though, after my visit to his office.'

Callum winced. 'You've been to see Dr Langton?'

'I have.'

'Was that wise?'

'I've no idea. It felt pretty good to me at the time.' She sent him a thoughtful glance. 'Have you come here to discuss my actions, or are you looking for a rundown on the latest management diktats and offerings?'

He frowned. 'And what would they be?'

She braced her shoulders. 'Here, I have a list. Perhaps you'd like to give me your opinion.' She pushed a piece of paper across the table to him.

'From now on, the pharmacist is going to pass to me any requests for prescription drugs that don't fit the criteria of generic or are expensive where cheaper versions are available. No more trying to sneak around the protocol and think it won't be noticed.'

He had the grace to look uncomfortable at that and she gave him a wry smile before going on. 'Another change that's about to happen—the cleaning contract was put out to tender, and a new team will be starting next week. I'm hoping everyone will do their best to make them welcome. And the cafeteria and restaurant likewise—they are being operated under new budgetary restrictions. But I'm sure people will find the meals just as nutritious and satisfying as before.'

She hesitated briefly, letting her words sink in. 'So, what do you think?'

He studied the paper in silence for a moment or two, and then said flatly, 'And those are just the tip of the iceberg. There are several more items written down here.'

'True.'

He raised dark brows. 'I hardly know what to

say. I think you're formidable…like a steam-roller.'

'Well, that's good, isn't it?' She made a fleeting smile. 'I think I'm quite pleased about that.'

His mouth twisted. 'It wasn't intended as a compliment.'

She shrugged and made a face. 'Perhaps it's all in the eye of the beholder. Was there anything else I can help you with?'

He put up his hands as though to ward her off. 'I don't think so. I can see that you're not in an altogether receptive mood, and I guess this is quite enough for me to be going on with.'

He left the room and Alex slumped back in her chair. She stared at the door long after he had gone. She felt as though all the air had left her body, and now she was thoroughly deflated.

She was utterly alone. The one man who had promised to support her, to be there for her, had gone and left her to her own devices. It all came down to a question of loyalty, didn't it? And it was beginning to look as though that was something that was distinctly lacking in their relationship.

CHAPTER EIGHT

ALEX stayed in her office for another half an hour, ostensibly dealing with managerial tasks, until the sounds of activity beyond her door intruded on her and drew her back into the mainstream of activity. She started working her way through the list of paediatric admissions, and when she was satisfied that their treatment was under way and all the necessary tests had been done, she went over to the reception desk.

'This has just arrived with the latest batch of lab reports,' Callum said, passing her a sheet of paper. He looked at her cautiously, as though trying to assess her mood. 'It's the test results for young Rachel.'

'It's about time,' Alex acknowledged. 'When I checked on her in the assessment ward first thing, she was still very poorly. The antibiotics don't seem to have done much to help, but at least her temperature's down and she's had no more seizures.'

He nodded. 'According to this report she has viral meningitis and encephalitis, but at least now we can start her on antiviral medication. I'm proposing to use acyclovir.' He gave her a wry smile. 'Does that meet with your approval, or will the pharmacist be blacklisting me?'

She scowled. 'Let's not resort to childishness, shall we?'

His mouth twitched. 'Sorry, obviously you need a little longer to get yourself back in the right frame of mind. Maybe coffee would help?'

'Or perhaps getting on with the task in hand would do the trick.' Her grey eyes flashed with renewed vigour. She wasn't going to let him ply her with coffee and coax her into submission. 'Isn't there a patient waiting in treatment room three? A small child, so I guess that's probably one of mine.'

He nodded. 'I looked in on him earlier, and sent him for an X-ray. He should be back from there by now.'

She shot him a quick glance. 'Do you want to keep this case?'

He shook his head. 'I have to see a cardiac patient. Anyway, I'd better not get any more involved with young Kyle. His parents were bickering about the ruination of their holiday... I could feel myself getting hot under the collar at their attitude, so perhaps it would be better if you take over. I wouldn't trust myself not to say something untoward.'

Alex was astonished. 'Hot under the collar— you? That doesn't sound like the man I know. You're always calm and relaxed, no matter what happens.'

'Not this time. In fact, I may already have gone too far.'

She gave a wry smile. 'It looks as though we're both having one of those days.'

He nodded, and threw her a quick glance. 'It must be something in the air.' He picked up a chart. 'But, seriously, you have a different way of looking at things, and maybe you'll manage the situation better. Perhaps I could look in on you later, and see how things are going?'

'Okay.' She was glad to be able to get back to work. It was what she knew best, and while she was with her patients at least she didn't have time to think about annoying administrators or wonder about how Callum managed to get under her skin and cause her emotions to ebb and flow like mercury.

Her patient was a young boy, six years old, tousle haired, with tearful blue eyes. A nurse had placed a supportive sling around his arm, but he looked thoroughly miserable.

'I don't know what we're doing here,' his father told her. 'There's nothing wrong with him. He just had a bit of a fall, that's all. He should have been looking where he was going, and then he wouldn't have tripped over. Anyway, he's done it before, and he's been fine afterwards. His mother's mollycoddling him, insisting on bringing him here.'

'A bit of a fall that has left him unable to use his arm,' Alex remarked in a blunt tone. 'I believe that's something that needs investigating.' She glanced at the boy and saw that a single tear was sliding down his cheek. 'And I have to ask you to think carefully about what you're saying, Mr Dunbar,' she added quietly. 'Your son is obviously very upset. I'd prefer we keep things calm and try to soothe him as best we can while we find out what is wrong.'

'More mollycoddling.' He strode across the room and stood by the window as though to distance himself from proceedings.

Alex went over to the boy. 'Hello, Kyle,' she greeted him. 'I'm Dr Draycott, and I'm going to have a look at you and see what we can do to make you feel better.' She gave him a reassuring smile. 'Has the nurse given you something for the pain?'

He nodded. 'She gave me some tablets.'

'And are they helping?'

'Yes, a bit.'

'Hmm.' She gently examined his arm, frowning when she discovered she couldn't feel the distal pulse. It was possible that a major artery was being constricted. 'There's quite a bit of swelling there,' she said, 'so I think we'll give you some medicine to help bring that down. Just excuse me for a moment, while I go and find a nurse to organise it.' Once the inflammation had settled down, it was quite possible that the pulse would be restored. If not, she would have to apply forearm traction as an emergency measure.

Katie was with another patient, but she agreed to bring the medication as soon as she had finished. 'I'll be with you in a few minutes,' she said. 'We're rushed off our feet here.'

'I know. I appreciate what you're up against.'

Going back to Kyle, she found his father pacing the room impatiently. 'We've been here for hours,' he complained.

Alex checked the waiting-time log. 'An hour and a half, to be exact,' she murmured. 'And in that time Kyle has been assessed by the triage nurse, looked at by a doctor, received painkillers and has been to Radiology for an X-ray.'

His mouth flattened. 'We were supposed to be setting out to meet up with relatives,' he said, 'my brother and his wife and their children. We were already late to begin with. They're coming all the way from London. Can't you just give him some more painkillers that we can take along with us?

He's got his arm in a sling. Why do we have to hang around? What's the problem?'

Alex brought the image of the X-ray film up on the computer monitor. 'There's the problem,' she said, pointing to an area of bone around the elbow. 'It isn't very clear on this film, but I believe it's what we call a supracondylar fracture. These things can be quite complicated, and need careful attention.'

She examined the boy once more, worried that there might have been damage to nerves in the arm, or vascular injuries. She looked up as Katie came into the room, and smiled in acknowledgement before turning back to her patient. 'I'm going to ask another doctor to come and take a look at you, Kyle,' she said gently. 'He's a doctor who knows all about bones and joints and how to put them right.'

Kyle's father made an explosive sound of exasperation. 'Another doctor? What's going on here? You're a qualified doctor, aren't you? Or aren't you capable of deciding what to do about it yourself? It's not that difficult, is it? He's always falling over or getting into scrapes. It's never anything serious. It's just how he is. He's clumsy.'

Kyle's bottom lip began to tremble, and tears washed his eyes once more. Alex stood up. Enough was enough. 'I can see this is a trying time for you, Mr Dunbar,' she said, 'so I'm going to ask you to leave. Kyle is obviously upset and I'm afraid your attitude is not helping. Perhaps you would care to go and get a cup of coffee in the waiting room just across the corridor?'

'No, I wouldn't.' He glowered at her.

'No? Then I'm afraid you leave me no option but to call Security and have you removed,' she said, stepping closer to him and speaking quietly so that Kyle would not hear. 'Your son is in a great deal of discomfort, he has a broken elbow, which may require surgery, and I need to be able to concentrate on my work. I'm sure, when you've had time to think things over, you'll come to realise that your child's health and well-being is far more important than you being late for a meeting.' She studied him for a moment or two. 'So, have you made your decision? Which is it to be? Do I call Security?'

He face was a rigid mask as he turned away from her and walked briskly out of the door. He didn't even look back to see if his wife was following.

'I must apologise for my husband,' Mrs Dunbar said, hurriedly. She was a thin, fair-haired woman, with blue eyes and features that closely resembled those of her son. 'He's been under a lot of pressure lately, but I'm sure he'll calm down before too long. A whole lot of things have gone wrong today, and he's a little uptight about this meeting with his brother and his family. They haven't seen each other for some time.' She gave Alex a quick look. 'I hope it's all right if I stay?'

'Of course. I'm sure Kyle will be glad of it.'

Alex went over to the phone at the side of the room to call for an orthopaedic surgeon to come and look at Kyle's arm. Katie was smiling, and as she came alongside her to prepare the boy's medication, she said softly, 'That was very well done, Alex. You and Callum must be two of a kind. The only difference is that Callum wasn't going to call Security, he was going to do the job himself until the man backed down.' She shook her head. 'It makes you wonder why some people bother to have children.'

'That's true.' So Callum had squared up to him? She couldn't imagine him doing anything so aggressive. It was so unlike him.

Alex went back to her young patient. 'It looks as though you've broken a bone in your elbow, Kyle,' she told him, 'and things are a bit out of place there, so a doctor needs to put them right for you. I think what will probably happen is that Mr Adams will come along and fix things for you. He'll give you something to make you go to sleep, so that you won't feel anything while he does it.' She looked at him. 'Is there anything you'd like to ask me?'

He shook his head. 'I don't think so.'

'Okay.' She turned to his mother. 'What about you, Mrs Dunbar? Do you have any questions?'

'Only one, really…do you have any idea how long will it be before his arm is better?'

'I couldn't say for certain…it really depends what Mr Adams, the surgeon, makes of it…but it's a longish job. It could be up to twelve weeks before function is restored, and overall it might take six months before things are completely back to normal.'

'Oh, dear.' Mrs Dunbar put an arm gently around her son. 'Not to worry, Kyle. Everyone's going to take good care of you here.'

'But Dad doesn't believe me.' Kyle hiccupped and chewed at his lower lip, still distressed. 'He thinks I'm making it up.'

'And your dad's going to be very sorry when he realises that you've really hurt your arm.'

Callum came to see how things were going some time later when Mr Adams was making his assessment.

'Luckily, he's had nothing to eat or drink for a few hours,' the surgeon said, taking Alex and Callum to one side after he had spoken to Kyle's mother, 'so I'll see him up in Theatre in about half an hour. And we'll admit him for observation. I don't foresee any problems, but you never know with these things.'

'Thanks,' Alex said. 'I'll make the preparations.'

She left the room with Callum some time later, leaving the boy in Katie's capable hands.

Callum checked his watch. 'It's getting late. Shall we go and get some lunch? There's nothing urgent going on here, and you look as though you could do with getting away from the hospital for a while.' He glanced at her. 'You're a bit pale, and I guess being here isn't helping very much. I know a pub not too far from here where they do a great lasagne—their honey-glazed ham is delicious, too. What do you say?'

She thought it over, but prevaricated. 'It sounds good, but I'm waiting for news about my brother. He took a turn for the worse this morning, and I want to be on hand in case they get back to me.'

He sucked in a sharp breath, his blue gaze running over her features. 'Alex, I'm sorry. You didn't say a word… I wish you'd told me, instead of trying to cope on your own. What is it…his lungs? You said the doctors thought he was fighting an infection, didn't you?'

She nodded. 'But I think this is something more. The nurse said they were worried about him. She's going to let me know if there's any news.'

His mouth firmed. 'This is all the more reason

for you to get away for a while. I think you've had about as much as you can handle for one morning. The pub is only a ten-minute drive away. We'll come back the instant we hear anything.'

'And what about A and E? Oughtn't we to stay around?'

'You're entitled to a proper break. There's another consultant on duty, plus the registrar, and in any case, we can be reached by phone. Katie will let us know if she hears of anything major coming in. Besides, you're not even supposed to be on clinical duty this afternoon, are you? This is one of your management days, isn't it?'

'Yes, it's true.' She sighed. 'You know, I think you're right, I could really do with getting away for a while, but I can't help thinking it would be unwise to leave the hospital grounds right now. At the same time, I feel as though I'm on a rollercoaster ride, going up and down and round and round, and now, all of a sudden, I just want to get off.'

'Then that's exactly what you'll do.' He took hold of her arm and led the way along the corridor to the main doors, stopping off on the way at the main desk to tell the clerk where they were going. Alex felt a strange sense of relief that he was taking charge.

They walked out to the car park. 'You're positive it isn't far away?' she said, a frown creasing her brow.

'I am.' He held open the car door for her, and she slid into the passenger seat, leaning back against the soft leather upholstery, relaxing in the sheer opulence of this luxurious vehicle. It even smelled new, and she closed her eyes and breathed in the subtle fragrance of expensive leather and wax polish.

They drove for a while through the Quantocks, past heather-clad moorland and rolling hills, where sparkling streams meandered by scattered villages and small hamlets. Soon they reached a charming country inn, and Callum drew the car to a halt on the forecourt.

'It's lovely,' Alex said, stepping out of the car and gazing around in wonder. 'Just look at that open countryside. It's so peaceful.'

'I thought you'd like it. Come inside, and we'll see if we can find a table by the window. The service is pretty good here. You don't usually have to wait too long for your meal.'

Alex chose seared breast of chicken wrapped in bacon and served with a tangy sauce, creamed potatoes and vegetables, while Callum opted for the lasagne.

'They make the sauce for the lasagne with red wine, tomato and Italian seasoning, as well as onion and mushrooms,' he told her. 'It's delicious.' He dipped a fork into the lasagne and offered it to her. 'Here, have a taste. Tell me what you think.'

He slid the food into her mouth and she savoured it for a moment or two, conscious all the while of his gaze centred on the ripe curve of her mouth before it moved along the slender column of her throat.

'Mmm…you're right, it's lovely.' She sent him a quick, mischievous glance. 'You just did that to make me doubt my choice, didn't you?' She made a weighing action with her hands. 'Chicken and bacon on the one hand…lasagne on the other… What to do…what to do?'

'You've changed your mind?' He smiled.

'That's all right, I'll swap you, if you like. It really doesn't matter to me.' He began to push his plate towards her.

'No...no, really, I was just kidding.' She held up a hand to stop him. 'Keep it, please. I'm perfectly happy with what I've chosen.' She sent him a quizzical glance. 'Trouble is, you're not used to seeing me in a teasing mood, are you? You see me as straightforward, always concentrating on work. I expect you think I'm not capable of letting my hair down.'

He shook his head. 'I don't know about that. I think you could be absolutely fabulous at letting your hair down, given half a chance.' His eyes glinted, his gaze moving slowly over her, taking in the smooth line of her dress that clung where it touched. His glance lingered. 'That's definitely something I'd love to see...but unfortunately I get the feeling it's highly unlikely.'

Alex felt her cheeks flush with heat. She could imagine spending time with Callum, getting close to him, experiencing the thrill of being in his arms, knowing the touch of his hands on her body...but she was coming to realise that she wanted much more from him than just a passion-ate fling.

It had never happened to her before. There had never been anyone who had made her feel this way, but now she knew she wanted a relationship that would last.

But where Callum was concerned, wasn't that just a flight of fancy? She couldn't help feeling that in the long term she simply wasn't his kind of woman. He would never choose to spend his life with a career woman. His soul mate would be someone who was relaxed and tranquil, someone who could share his philosophy on life, instead of a woman who caused him problems on a daily basis.

'The trouble is,' he said, bringing her back to the present with a jolt, 'you never have time to simply be yourself.' He tasted the lasagne and was thoughtful for a moment. 'There are always too many demands on you…like this morning, for instance. You were plunged into that press conference out of the blue, and that's probably why you—'

He broke off, and Alex finished for him. 'That's

probably why I reacted the way I did this morn-ing.' She gave an awkward smile. 'I'm sorry about that. You were just doing what you felt to be right.'

'Still, it's perhaps just as well that we showed Dr Langton we wouldn't let him get his own way without a fight. He'll keep pushing it.' Callum paused, his fork halfway to his mouth. 'Anyway, what did you say to him? Did you ask him about the circular?'

She nodded. 'I told him that I had some propos-als of my own to put before the board.'

'Good.' He frowned. 'In fact, just before we came away, I heard he's organising a meeting with the board for tomorrow to bring it to a vote. That could turn out to be a turning point for all of us…but with you there to back our cause, I imagine we stand a better chance.'

'Maybe. Though, going on what we talked about the other day—renting out services, and so on—I've already put forward some money-spinning suggestions to the board in the emails I sent out. They won't be popular with everyone, but I'm hoping they'll at least have time to think about them.' She took a sip of her iced drink, a pure fruit juice topped up with lemonade. 'It all depends whether they agree with my way of thinking…but either way, I don't see how we can do any more.'

He curled some creamy strands of cheese around his fork. 'We could try to get a licence to run a lottery. That should bring in quite a bit of money for the department, and there are always raffles to be run every now and again. I'm on the fundraising committee and we have some good people who are willing to put in a lot of time and effort for the cause.'

'They get results, too, judging by the new portable X-ray machine we've just acquired.' Her mouth curved. 'You're not at all what you seem, are you? You appear to be quiet and un-assuming and altogether laid-back, but one way and another you achieve an awful lot behind the scenes, don't you? I'm thinking about the way the doctors and nurses look up to you and respect your decisions…and then there are those seri-ously ill patients you manage to edge higher up the waiting lists, not to mention the way you handle the press.'

He made a dismissive movement with his hands. 'What's the point of being in high places if you can't manipulate the odds from time to time?'

She chuckled and finished off her chicken and bacon, laying down her knife and fork.

'Would you like dessert and coffee?' he asked, and she nodded.

'Oh, yes, please. I've had my eye on the toffee pudding they have in the glass-fronted display case over there. And coffee would be great, thanks.' She toyed with her serviette while he called the waitress over to take their order.

'I'll have the apple pie,' he said, handing the girl the menus. She nodded, giving him a dimpled smile, and he responded with a gentle curve of his lips.

Watching them, Alex felt an immediate, involuntary stab of jealousy. The force of it shocked her to the core. What was wrong with her? Why did it matter that he smiled at a girl in a restaurant? She frowned. The truth was, she was beginning to care for him deeply, but how could she ever compete with all those pretty girls who knew how to take life as it came and simply enjoy being around a good-looking, easygoing man?

She didn't know how to be his type of woman. She was here with him now, enjoying a wonderful meal in a romantic country inn, and hadn't she spent most of the time talking about work?

Callum glanced at her, a small line indenting his brow. 'Is everything all right? You look anxious all at once.'

'I'm fine.' She tried to get a grip on herself. He was too perceptive by half and it wouldn't do to have him know what she was thinking. 'I'm glad you brought me here,' she said. 'It's good to be able to relax and enjoy the comfort, and the great food, as well as to look out over the hills. It just makes me wish I could do it more often. Of course, it's difficult with the children.'

He nodded. 'You could always bring them with you...except I don't suppose you'd be able to relax too much, knowing how those two get into everything.' He sent her a crooked grin. 'They certainly keep you on your toes.'

'True.'

He shot her a quick look. 'You must be really pleased with the way things are shaping up at home. The trees in the orchard look healthy and strong, and it looks as though it will be a good crop. But I still can't imagine how you settled on such a place. I could see you in a small, executive-type home, with all the mod-cons, something easy to manage, with no fripperies, but I've never picked out a rambling farmhouse with acres of land, in a month of Sundays.'

'You see me living a very orderly life, don't you?' She smiled. 'I must say, nothing's been straightforward these last few months. Far from it. I've had to come to terms with a whole new way of life, but I've found that I'm actually enjoying the farmhouse side of it. It's the one place where I feel contented. I think the children are happier for being there, too.'

'Where will they live when your brother and his wife come home from hospital? Didn't you say they used to rent a place before the accident?'

'That's right. Ross had relocated because of his job, and was renting while he looked around for something suitable. I expect they'll do the same again.'

She studied him. 'But what about you? I haven't seen your house, but I imagine you living in something like a barn conversion, with lots of books and a plasma TV and music centre.'

He laughed. 'Completely wrong, I'm afraid. I have what they call a studio apartment not too far from the hospital. I don't need anything grand, because it's just me living there. It's basically open plan, with a mezzanine floor where I have my bed…and my books. There are definitely lots of books.'

'And the building work you mentioned a while back?'

'I had the garage extended, and a wall built around the back of the garden. It's only small piece of land, but it goes with the apartment, and I wanted to keep it secluded.'

She shook her head, trying to imagine how he lived. 'That's not at all what I expected,' she said. 'You drive a fantastic car, you wear expensive, beautifully tailored clothes, and I expected your house would be equally grand.'

He shrugged. 'When I bought it, some years back, I didn't see the point in owning anything more than a bachelor pad. Not that it's under par in any way… I've been told it has the wow factor that everyone goes on about these days. But the fact is, I was young and I didn't see any reason to settle down, start a family and so on. I suppose I looked at the way my parents lived their lives and decided that maybe marriage and commit- ment weren't for me. My parents were never in one place for long and, no matter how they tried, they weren't able to look after me properly.'

'Not all families are like that.'

'No.' He winced. 'But you see those like the Dunbars, where everything is supposedly normal and yet beneath the surface there are all those tensions bubbling away…a father who thinks more of his own agenda, rather than caring for his son. I wonder sometimes if they're represen- tative of a good many families. I don't know. I just see so many broken relationships, children left without steady parenting, and it makes me think that's not the sort of thing I would want for myself.'

Alex didn't comment on that. She didn't know what to say. Instead, she dipped her spoon into her toffee pudding and let it rest there for a moment or two. Callum had said he didn't want marriage or commitment—or at least, that's how he had felt when he'd first bought the apartment, and yet she'd come to realise that those were the very things she wanted. All these years, she'd been relaxed about how she viewed relationships, but things had changed. She'd met Callum, and she'd discovered that for her, it was all or nothing.

If he was still keen on the bachelor way of life, it seemed that she had been right to be cautious about getting involved. Trouble was, it was way too late for that now.

CHAPTER NINE

'OH, GOOD, you're back.' Katie greeted Alex and Callum as they walked into A and E after spending their lunch break. 'Your niece and nephew arrived a few minutes ago with your neighbour, Alex—she said her name was Martha. I'm afraid the children are a bit upset—they've been asking for you. I suggested they might like to wait in the staff lounge. I thought it would be a bit more comfortable for them in there.'

'Thanks, Katie. That was thoughtful of you.' Alex's heart had started hammering, going into alarm mode at the news, but she tried to stay calm as she asked, 'Do you happen to know what they're upset about? Is it my brother?'

Katie nodded. 'I think so. It sounds as though he's in a bad way and they weren't expecting to see him like that. The nurse didn't realise they'd gone in to see him until it was too late.'

Alex took a steadying breath. 'I'll go and see if I can smooth things over. Thanks again, Katie.'

'You're welcome. I found them some paper and coloured pencils, and one or two toys to try to keep them occupied for a while, but I don't think they can settle to anything.'

Alex nodded. 'I knew I should have stayed here,' she said under her breath. 'I just knew something would go wrong.'

Callum laid a restraining hand on her arm. 'Don't start blaming yourself,' he advised her. 'Take a deep breath and stay calm. You had lunch, nothing more, and they've only been here for a few minutes. You can't be at everyone's beck and call every minute of the day. They'll come through this. You'll all come through it.'

'I'm all right.' She was beginning to feel increasingly agitated. 'I must go.'

'I'd like to come with you. Is that okay? I might be able to help in some way.'

She nodded, and they hurried along to the staff lounge.

They found Sarah in tears, sitting on one of the sofas, while James was trying to keep a stiff upper lip but was unable to disguise his shaky, ragged intakes of breath. He looked at Alex with bewildered eyes, not really knowing what was going on but sensing the tense, unhappy atmosphere in the room.

'I feel terrible about this,' Martha said, coming to meet Alex. She was a sensible woman, middle-aged, with gently waving brown hair and grey eyes that were troubled. 'I'd no idea Ross was in such a bad way or I'd never have taken them to see him.'

'What happened?' Alex tried to suppress her anxiety, wanting to stay calm and composed for the sake of the children. 'Did the nurse tell you what was going on?'

Martha shook her head. 'She wouldn't tell me anything about his condition, because I'm not a relative.' She lowered her voice. 'But he looked terrible…pale, with beads of sweat on his face, not breathing properly. He was very weak.'

'Daddy couldn't talk to me,' Sarah said, the tears welling up in her eyes and spilling over. 'He couldn't sit up in bed or do anything. And the nurse had to help him lean back against his pillows.' Her voice began to wobble. 'I tried to talk to him, but he couldn't answer me. His mouth moved but nothing came out and then the nurse put a mask on his face.' She began to sob.

Alex went to sit down on the sofa between the two children. She put her arms around Sarah and held her close. 'I'm sorry you had to see your dad looking so poorly,' she said softly. 'I know the doctors and nurses are doing everything they can to make him better.'

Sarah's sobs became louder. 'But it's not working.'

Alex hugged her, and laid an arm around James's shoulders, squeezing him gently. He, too, had given way to tears. 'Have you been to see your mother?' she asked.

James nodded. 'We gave her the flower basket.' He pulled in a shuddery breath. 'She said she thought it was lovely.'

'That's good, isn't it? You know, she's doing so well, I expect she'll be coming home soon. You'll like that, won't you?'

'Yes. She said she'd be home in a few days. She

wants to come and live at your house for a bit.'
He looked up at her. 'Can she?'

'Yes, of course.' She glanced at Sarah to see if
any of their conversation had managed to divert
her, but the little girl was locked into a cycle of
misery.

'I think I should take them home,' Martha said
quietly. 'They wanted to stay here and see you,
or we would have gone earlier.'

'I know. Thanks, Martha.'

Sarah turned tear-drenched eyes on Alex. 'I
want you to come home with us.'

'I'll come in a little while, Sarah.' She glanced
at her watch. 'I have to finish my shift here, just
another couple of hours, and then I'll be home
with you.'

It wasn't what she wanted to hear, and Sarah
started to cry all over again.

Callum went down on his haunches beside her.
'You know, Sarah,' he said in a quiet voice, 'your
mother wouldn't want you to be upset like this.
She'd want you to be strong, so that you can take
care of your little brother. He doesn't really understand what's going on, but if he sees you being

all grown up and getting on with things, it will be better for all of you.' He paused, waiting to see what effect his words were having on her. 'Maybe you could go home and start preparing a room for your mother. Put some flowers in it, perhaps make up a fruit basket, or make something for her that she'll enjoy when she comes home.'

'Like a little box for her rings?' James's eyes lit up with enthusiasm. 'We did some paper curling at school...we could make a lid with some decorations on it.'

'They call it quilling, I think,' Martha said. 'I've some coloured paper we can use. Shall we go home and give it a try?'

James nodded, wanting to go right away and get started, but Sarah was still reticent. 'I don't want you to stay at work,' she said, looking earnestly at Alex. 'I want you to come home with us.'

Callum stood up, laying a gentle hand on her shoulder. 'She won't be long.'

'I'll be there before you know it,' Alex told her. 'Go home with Martha now, and I'll follow in my car. I won't be long, I promise.'

They left a few minutes later, with James full of ideas about the box he was going to make and Sarah still subdued. Alex watched them go and then, as the strength drained out of her body, she reached for a chair and sank down into it.

'You know, you could have gone with them,' Callum murmured. 'You don't have to stay here, and it's obvious they need you. Sarah must have been very shocked by what she saw, and she clearly needs reassurance—perhaps that's something only you can give her. Martha's doing her best, but she isn't a relative. The children have already gone through the distress of knowing their parents were injured in a road accident, and now this is an added stressor.'

'Do you think I don't know that?' She resented his implied criticism. 'Do you imagine all I ever think about is work? I want to be with them, I want to make all this go away, but I can't.'

Perhaps she had been too sharp in her retort, because his head went back a fraction, light flaring in his blue eyes, his mouth making a straight line, and she was instantly conscious of the fact that he was only trying to help. The last thing she needed right now was to get into an argument with Callum.

'I have to go and see my brother and find out what's gone wrong,' she said. She felt as though she was caught up in the middle of a whirlwind. These last few months had been a nightmare and she was about at the end of her tether. Her brother was dangerously ill and she needed to go to him. He was her priority right now.

'Of course you do.' He frowned. 'But I don't think you should be on your own right now. I want to be there with you.'

A feeling of relief shot through her at his understanding. She gave a faint, almost imperceptible nod, and they left the room together.

When they arrived at the intensive care unit Alex found that her brother was every bit as ill as Martha had said.

'He looks so much worse than he did this morning,' she said in a whisper, and Callum laid a comforting arm around her shoulders. It was plain to see that Ross was in a bad way. He was deathly pale, and the constant bleeping of the monitors around him warned of a galloping heart rate and a worrying lack of oxygen in his blood.

'We've been doing tests all morning,' the nurse told her, 'but Dr Allingham looked at the CT scan a little while ago and said he has a pulmonary embolism. I was just about to page you.'

Alex pulled in a shaky breath. A blood clot on the lung was a dreadful diagnosis. Depending on its severity, it could mean the difference between life and death, and, judging by Ross's condition, this was the worst news she could have received. A blood clot in one of the main arteries could cause his circulation to fail, and the damage to his lungs would mean he couldn't get enough oxygen to his tissues.

'What is Dr Allingham going to do?'

'He started him straight away on anticoagulants, and he's prescribed thrombolytic therapy. It will take a while, of course, but he's hoping that we'll see initial results within the next twenty-four hours. After all Ross has been through, he wants to reserve surgery as a last option.'

'I can understand that.'

She looked at Callum, her eyes bright with

tears, and he said softly, 'They're doing everything they can for him. At least they've found out
what's wrong, and now they can do something
about it.'

'I know.' It didn't make it any easier to bear,
though. Who could say if the medication would
work quickly enough? Anticoagulants would thin
his blood and prevent any more clots from form-
ing, while the thrombolytic therapy would begin
to dissolve the clot, but this was a race against
time.

Callum gently drew her head down into the
crook of his shoulder, and she nestled against
him for a moment or two, absorbing the comfort
he offered. Tears trickled down her cheeks, but
she was soothed by his steady support. He was
strong and reliable, and by being with her right
now he was showing her that he cared about her
and her brother.

After a while she managed to gather herself
together. She glanced at the nurse. 'I'd like to
stay with him for a while, if that's all right?'

The girl nodded. 'Of course.'

She stayed with Ross for a few minutes, talking

to him even though she couldn't be sure that he heard her. She told him how Beth was becoming stronger, day by day, and how the children were looking forward to him coming home. 'You've always been a fighter, Ross,' she said softly. 'You can do it. You can get through this.'

When she was ready to go, she walked with Callum to the car park. 'I could drive you home,' he said, but she shook her head.

'I'll be all right. Thank you for staying with me.'

'I wanted to be with you.' He hesitated. 'Maybe when your brother is better and things are going more smoothly for you, we could spend some time together...maybe take a trip somewhere. I think it will do you a world of good.'

She nodded. 'Maybe.'

The children were quiet when she picked them up from Martha's house and took them home. James, being younger, was vaguely aware that something bad was happening, but it wasn't at the forefront of his mind. He could be distracted fairly easily. Sarah was much more difficult to handle. She was a sensitive, loving child, and intelligent enough to recognise that her father was in great danger. She'd always been Daddy's girl, and this was hard for her to take in. She knew there was a chance that he might not come through this latest setback.

'Shall we do some baking?' Alex suggested when they were back in the farmhouse kitchen. 'I thought we might make an apple-and-blackberry pie and take it round to Auntie Jane. She's only just home from hospital, so she's not up to doing very much for herself yet. I expect she'd be glad of some home cooking.'

Sarah nodded, and James went to fetch the pastry board and rolling pin. 'I love apple-and-blackberry pie,' he said. 'Do you think we'd better make two?'

'Definitely. That's a very good idea.'

By keeping them busy, Alex managed to calm them down over the next few hours, but she wasn't at all sure how she was going to handle things the next day. Instinct told her she should stay home with them, but she was supposed to be on duty at the hospital and Dr Langton had called a crucial meeting for the afternoon.

'Are you going to work today?' Sarah asked her at breakfast next morning. Her expression gave nothing away, but she didn't quite look Alex in the eye, and there was the merest flicker of a glance from under her lashes as she tried to gauge Alex's response.

Alex hesitated. 'I thought I'd stay here with you,' she said. 'We could go and see Auntie Jane this morning, and perhaps we might plant those dahlias for her—the ones that she bought before she went into hospital. And of course there will be a lot of weeding to do.'

'Yay! I want to do that,' James said, cramming a piece of buttered toast into his mouth.

Sarah relaxed visibly, her shoulders sloping as though a great weight had been lifted from her. She came over to Alex and gave her a hug. 'Can we phone Mummy later today? I want to tell her about the room we're getting ready for her and Daddy. She said Gran and Grandad were going to visit her this afternoon, so I might be able to talk to them as well.'

'Okay. That sounds like a good idea. It's good

that your gran and grandad have been able to come to see them, isn't it?'

Sarah nodded. 'They said they wanted to see me and James as well. Grandad said his job was all done and they were coming back to stay at their house in Somerset.'

'That's good news, isn't it? I expect they'll come and see both of you very soon.'

In the meantime, Alex was still in a quandary about work. She wasn't sure what she was going to do about Dr Langton's meeting, but the least she could do was to warn Callum that she wouldn't be there. She called him after she had rung the hospital for an update on her brother.

'I'm going to stay at home with the children today, and probably tomorrow as well,' she told him. 'I think it's for the best.'

'I wondered what you would do,' he said. 'Is everything all right? Are they okay?'

'They seem to be,' she said. It was good to hear his deep voice. It was somehow reassuring, as though he was close to her even though the miles separated them. 'They're a lot more settled, having me here with them. Things are probably a lot better all round this way. Dr Langton seems to think so, anyway. That's the impression I had when I spoke to him on the phone a few minutes ago. I get the feeling he's pleased I won't be there to spike his guns.'

'Hmm. How do you feel about that?'

She was quiet for a moment. 'A bit deflated, really, and anxious because I might be letting people down. But I don't see any way round the situation. Sarah's not saying very much, but she's on the verge of tears a lot of the time, and what she's not saying is speaking volumes, if you know what I mean.'

'Yes, I think I do. I can understand why you've chosen to stay with them. As to the meeting, it's a pity I'm not on the committee, or I could stand in for you and state your case. Let me give it some thought, and I'll see if there's some way we can get round it.'

'Thanks, Callum.' She didn't think there was anything much he could do, but she was glad of his offer to help. He was without exception caring and thoughtful, ready to step in where he was needed, and she was coming to realise that he was someone she could rely on in her darkest hour.

'I'm happy to do what I can,' he said. 'Is there any news about Ross?'

'Only that his condition is much the same. At least he isn't any worse. I haven't told Beth yet. I didn't want to worry her, and I'm hoping Sarah won't say anything when she phones her this afternoon. I'd sooner tell her if and when he appears to be on the mend.'

'That sounds reasonable enough to me. Keep your chin up. Just remember I'm here for you if you need me.'

'I will. Thanks.' She was sad when he cut the call, because she wanted to go on hearing his voice. It filled the empty void and made her feel that she was not alone, just for a few minutes. She wanted to be with him.

In truth though, wasn't she kidding herself? He was concerned about her and he was offering to help, but what did he really feel about her? Yes, he was caring and sympathetic, and he had shown her that he would be there for her, but how deep did his feelings go? He might be attracted to her, but that might be as far as it went.

And who was she to complain about that? Wasn't that how she had viewed things, to begin with? Her career meant everything to her, and there had never been much time for anything else. She had been reasonably content. There had been no one who might have persuaded her to set it all aside...until now, until she had met Callum. He had proved himself to be a man apart from all others. He was quiet, strong and steady, and he had tried to show her how to take herself less seriously.

And perhaps his efforts had achieved a result. After all, she had changed over these last few months. Perhaps looking after her brother's children had shown her a different way of life, had taught her that home and family could take precedence over ambition.

She sighed. Musing on all this wasn't getting her anywhere. For now, she had to put aside her thoughts about Callum and concentrate on the children. They needed her, and she ought to be keeping them occupied instead of standing here wool-gathering.

'We need the gardening tools,' she told them, calling them back into the kitchen a few minutes later. 'Gardening gloves, forks, trowels and the bag of plant food out of the greenhouse. We'll need compost, too.'

'I'll get the food,' James said. 'Sarah can bring the tools.'

'I'm not carrying all that lot on my own,' Sarah complained, scowling at her younger brother. 'You can help.'

'Nah.'

He threw her a mutinous, cheeky glance and ran off, leaving Sarah to say crossly, 'He's always doing that. Daddy says he… Daddy said—' She broke off, biting her lip to stop it from trembling, and Alex put her arms around her and gave her a hug.

'I'll help you with the tools. I'll talk to James in a little while—just as soon as I manage to catch him,' she said.

They spent the morning with Jane, planting dahlias in her sunny border, while she sat in a garden chair and offered them cold drinks from an iced jug.

'You look so much better than you did a while ago,' Alex told her, coming to sit beside her and take a break for a while. 'Has your blood pressure settled down yet?'

Jane nodded. 'Yes, it has. And I'm healing up nicely, too, so I'm beginning to feel as though I'm on the mend at last.'

'That's really good news.' Alex took a long swallow from her glass. 'That was a bit of a scare you had, back in the hospital, wasn't it? I know Callum was worried about you.'

'He's a good man. He's always looked out for me, and made sure that I was getting on all right.' Jane was quiet for a moment or two, and Alex guessed she was thinking about the way he had helped her over the years. 'I know he has a difficult job to do at the hospital, and sometimes he has a lot on his mind, with all the worries about patients, and so on. He cares about people, you see. And I know he's concerned about these threats to close the unit down. He said he'd written to the board members, telling them of the risks to patients if services were to be transferred to the city.'

'Has he?' Alex was surprised. 'He didn't mention that to me.'

'No, well, I think he feels you have enough to cope with already. He didn't want you worrying about what he was doing and saying.'

Perhaps he had been put off by her reaction when he'd gone to the press. Alex made a face. It was her own fault that he didn't confide in her. Just lately she had been edgy and out of sorts, and who could blame him for going it alone?

Still, he'd offered to try to sort something out before the meeting this afternoon. Would he be able to come up with anything? She wanted to put her views to the board, and it would have been much better to do that in person rather than through an email that some members might not even have read.

She took the children back home an hour or so later. 'Why don't you go and play in the orchard for a bit while I make lunch?' she suggested.

'I want to stay here, with you,' Sarah said quietly. 'I don't want to play. Do you think Daddy is all right?' Her voice quavered. 'I heard the nurse say that he might not make it without an operation.'

Alex frowned, and Sarah hurried to add, 'She didn't know I was there. She was talking to another nurse.'

Alex studied her thoughtfully. She had been clingy all morning, not wanting to stray far from her side, and that made her realise that it was probably a wise decision she had made to stay home with her. What was it Callum had said? The children needed a relative at a time like this. 'I'm sorry you heard that,' she said. 'It must have been upsetting for you, but the nurse said she would ring me if there was any news about your father—if he had taken a turn for the worse. Even so, I'm going to phone her now, to find out what's happening. After that, you can talk to your mum, if you like.'

Sarah nodded. James took himself off to the garden to play on the old rope swing, and Alex dialled the hospital number. Best to do it now, and hopefully put Sarah's mind at ease, along with her own.

'There's been no major change,' the nurse told her, 'but his blood oxygen level has risen very slightly. Dr Allingham thinks that could be a good sign, but he says Ross has quite a way to go yet.'

'Thanks.' Alex relayed the news to Sarah. 'It means we still have to wait and see, but at least it's not bad news.' It was difficult to know how to handle this kind of situation with a young child. She didn't want to be negative, but at the same time she didn't want to fill Sarah with false hope. The consequences of that could turn out to be disastrous.

She left Sarah talking to her mother and grand-parents a few minutes later, and went into the kitchen to prepare a salad for lunch. Her mobile rang as she was slicing peppers, and she wiped her hands on a towel and went to answer it.

'Hi, there,' Callum said, and her heart warmed at the sound of his voice. 'How are things? Are you managing all right with the children? Are they coping?'

'James is fine,' she answered, 'but Sarah's find-ing things difficult. We just rang the hospital to see how Ross was doing and there's been no real change as yet.'

'These things take time. At least they've made the diagnosis and started to act on it. A good many pulmonary embolisms go undetected until it's too late.'

'I know.'

'And how are you? Are you bearing up?'

'I'm okay.' She wasn't going to tell him how she really felt, her worries about her brother or her fears for the children's well-being. For the moment, it was enough for her that he had called. His voice was deep and soothing, like a balm to her overwrought senses.

If only he could be here with her right now. Suddenly, she wanted to see him, to be with him. She wanted to have him hold her and reassure her that everything was going to turn out all right. Just being in his arms would have given her the strength to go on.

'How about you?' she asked. 'Your aunt said you were concerned about what was going on at the hospital. She said you'd written to the board.'

'That's true. I thought it might help. Actually,

I've been thinking about the meeting this afternoon, and I've a suggestion to put to you. You don't have to consider it…you might have other plans, or you might want to walk away from it all, given that you've so much on your plate right now.' She could hear the frown in his voice. 'Though I think you should know that most of the staff appreciate how hard you've worked ever since you started the job and they're all behind you in this.'

'I'm glad about that. What was it you wanted to ask me?'

'It occurred to me that you could still take part in the meeting if we set up a video link. I could fix it from the hospital end—it would give me an excuse to be in on the meeting if I have to monitor the link, so I could maybe add my twopenny worth to anyone who cares to listen. And anyway the executives have asked for one or two representatives from non-board members to be present—and you could set up the software and web-cam on your laptop from your end.'

She thought about it for a while. Having Callum take part in the meeting was another bonus point.

'It sounds feasible, but I don't know how well it would go down with the board if Sarah or James were to come and interrupt every few minutes.'

He chuckled. 'That's one of the hazards of working from home, I suppose. You could always bribe them to keep quiet with fizzy pop and cookies. Not very politically correct, but quite effective at times, I'm told.'

'Yes, you're probably right.' She came to a decision after a second or two. 'I dare say I'll think of something. Will you let me know when you've organised it at your end?'

'I will.' There was a smile in his voice. 'Thanks, Alex. I owe you one.'

'Let's just hope it goes well. I'll do my best, but I can't promise anyone will listen.'

He rang off, and Alex went on with her preparations for lunch, trying to think of ways to keep the children amused while she attended the virtual meeting.

'How about you look through the DVD collection and choose something to watch while I'm talking to the people at work?' she suggested, taking the easy way out. 'I really need you to promise not to interrupt me unless it's something very important. Do you think you can do that?'

'Yeah…if we can watch space aliens,' James announced eagerly.

'Space aliens are rubbish,' Sarah told him. 'We should watch the one about the animals who escape from the farm.'

'Nah…that's a girly film. I'm not watching a girly film.'

Alex intervened. 'You have five minutes to choose something you both agree on,' she said briskly, 'or I'll choose for you.'

Half an hour later, she was seated at her desk in the study, talking to the hospital executives. Callum's image appeared on her computer monitor, almost centrally on her screen, and it was a huge comfort to her to be able to see him, even if he was not there with her in the flesh.

'You already know of the many savings we've made in the A and E department,' she said, addressing the board in general. 'We've gone almost as far as we can down that route. Perhaps the time has come to think of the situation from another angle.'

'Another angle?' one of the executives chal-
lenged her. 'What are you suggesting?'

'I think we could look at ways to bring money
into the hospital.'

He frowned. 'And how do you propose to do
that?'

'There are some areas that are underused for
one reason or another. I'm suggesting that we
could rent out certain wards and theatres to the
private sector. There's also the scanner—it isn't
used from six o'clock in the evening unless there
is an emergency—and it seems to me that's another opportunity for us to earn income from
the private sector. Fee-paying patients will benefit from having treatment out of hours, and the
hospital will gain by getting a badly needed cash
boost.'

'This is the NHS,' Dr Langton said dismis-
sively. 'The principle has always been that it is
free for those in need of medical help. NHS treatment and private medicine don't mix. The two
are incompatible.'

Alex nodded. 'I know some people find the
idea of private medicine unpalatable. I've always

believed in the principle of the NHS, that treatment should be free for everyone who needs it. But the private sector serves a purpose for those who don't want to wait to see a specialist or be put on a long waiting list for surgery, and in these days of cash-strapped hospitals perhaps this is the time for radical thinking. A good many hospitals have already gone along this route, with great success. With the money earned from the private sector, we could keep the department open and make changes that would benefit other areas of the hospital.'

Callum intervened. 'I think Alex is right. With extra money we could streamline some of the services we already offer and make them more efficient. We could set up a minor injuries unit to be run by nurses and a doctor—maybe a GP—and we could add a new mini-stroke unit, which would have a preventative role and eventually save patients from progressing to major problems—which in themselves would cause further strain on our limited resources.'

The discussion went on for another hour before Dr Langton drew the meeting to a close.

'Thank you, everyone,' he said. 'Obviously, a lot of points have been made here today, and they will need some consideration. I suggest that the executive board meets again tomorrow to make its final decision.'

Alex gazed at the screen. She had done what she could and now they simply had to wait for the result.

Callum's glance meshed with hers. His expression mirrored her thoughts, saying, 'That's it for now. There's nothing more we can do.'

She looked for something extra in his eyes, something that would show her a hidden message, perhaps, a hint that he wanted to be with her...but there was nothing. He simply turned away as one of the executives began to speak to him, and a few minutes later the video link was cut.

CHAPTER TEN

ALEX wandered aimlessly about the house next day, trying to decide which job she ought to do next. Nothing appealed to her or filled her with enthusiasm. The trouble was, she didn't feel inclined to do anything. All she really wanted was to talk to Callum, to hear his voice. Better still, she would have liked to be with him.

She reached for the phone before she could change her mind. 'Hi, Callum,' she said. 'I hope you don't mind me disturbing you at work. Are you busy?'

'Alex…' She could hear the smile in his voice. 'You can call me at any time. In fact, I was about to call you myself. It's quiet here just now…no major accidents, just a waiting room full of the walking wounded. Of course, we're all waiting for news of the board meeting, but we won't get that until a little later.' Then he added on a concerned note, 'Anyway, how are you? Are you all right?'

'Yes, I'm fine. I just…' She let the words trail off. Perhaps it had been a mistake to call him—she never made the first move with any man, and she was acting completely out of character—but for once she had thrown caution to the wind. 'I'm on my own here,' she said, 'and I just wanted to talk to you for a while…not about anything in particular.'

'You're on your own? How did that come about?'

'My parents came over just before lunch and took the children out for the afternoon.'

'That's brilliant,' Callum said. 'You must be glad of the break.'

'Yes, it's lovely for the children to be able to go out with their grandparents. The thing is, Mum and Dad are back here to stay now, in Somerset, and they say they'll be around to help out from now on…which is great news. I just wasn't expecting it and, to be honest, I'm not used to having the place to myself. I'm feeling a little strange…a bit lost, somehow. I know that must sound odd.'

'It doesn't sound odd at all to me. You've been through a difficult time lately, and you're used to working at full stretch.' He chuckled. 'It isn't every day you get the chance to play hooky.'

'No.' She smiled. 'I suppose not.'

He sobered. 'Is there any news about Ross?'

'Yes,' she said brightly. 'They say they're cautiously optimistic. His oxygen levels are better and his breathing is a little easier. Actually, I was thinking of going in to see him in a while.'

'That's a good idea. It will cheer you up to see him looking better.' The smile was back in his voice. 'Maybe I could go with you? I could come and pick you up, and then we can play hooky together?'

She laughed. 'But you're at work…are you saying you're going to take time off? That isn't like you.'

'No, it isn't,' he agreed. 'But I have a half-day owing to me, and it seems to me that this is as good a time as any to take it. Besides, I want to make sure that you're all right.'

'I am, thanks.'

'Good. Well, perhaps after you've been to see Ross, we could go out for the afternoon and make the most of the sunshine. What do you say?'

'I'd like that…if you're sure you can get away.'

'I can. I'll come and pick you up in half an hour.'

She was glowing inside when she cut the call a second or two later. She looked around. It was only just dawning on her that everything she'd done, all the loving care she'd poured into this place was for nothing if she didn't have Callum by her side. And now her dreams were coming true because he was on his way home to her.

The doorbell rang some half an hour later, and she hurried to answer it.

'Hi,' Callum said, as she pulled open the door. He rested a hand against the doorpost and gave her an engaging grin.

She couldn't stop the smile from spreading across her face. 'I was half-afraid you would change your mind,' she said. 'I thought if an emergency cropped up you'd have to stay at the hospital.'

He shook his head. 'We've enough people on duty to cover this afternoon.' He sniffed the air. 'Is that coffee I can smell?'

'Yes, come in, and I'll get it for you.'

He followed her into the kitchen. He looked like perfection to her, long and lean and totally masculine, wearing dark trousers that moulded his long legs and a cotton shirt that was open at the neck to give a glimpse of lightly bronzed skin.

She passed him a mug, and he sipped the hot liquid as he glanced around. 'It's very quiet in here without the children. I don't know whether that's a good thing or a bad thing. I think I could get used to the sound of their banter.'

'Me, too. I've loved having them around.'

'Still, it gives us the chance to slip away, doesn't it? After we've called in at the hospital, I thought we might take a trip to Cheddar Gorge and see the sights if you want?'

She nodded, her spirits soaring. 'I'd like that.'

'Good. Maybe we'll have lunch when we get there, and then take a wander around the place?

I don't know how you feel about exploring the caves, but the whole area is beautiful.'

'So I've heard.' It didn't really matter to her where they went. Just being with him was enough for now.

They called in at the hospital a short time later. Ross was still being given supplemental oxygen, and he was breathing faster than normal, but he was propped up against his pillows and he was able to talk to them, which filled Alex with hope.

'It's good to see you, Alex,' Ross said, taking his time with the words. His grey eyes were filled with warmth. 'I feel we owe you so much, Beth and I.'

'No, you don't.' She glanced at the monitors, glad to see that the readings were coming down to a more normal level. She could hardly believe that this was the man who had been so near to death a couple of days ago. 'I'm just so happy to see you looking so much better than before. Has Dr Allingham been in to see you today?'

'Yes, he came just about an hour ago. He seemed pleased.' He rested for a few moments, leaning his head back against his pillows, a lock of brown hair falling across his brow. Alex looked at him with affection. 'He said there was a chance I might go home in a couple of weeks if I go on making progress. I'll have to carry on with the medication for a few months, but he thinks I'll be able to build up my strength better at home.'

'That's brilliant news.' Alex gave him a hug. 'I told Beth you could all stay at my house until you find a place of your own. You haven't seen it yet, but I know you'll like it. There's plenty of room. It's an old farmhouse I bought, with extensions that have been added on over the years.'

'Thanks for that, Alex. You're a treasure.' He glanced at Callum, who was standing quietly by her side. 'I don't think I've seen you before, have I? You must be someone special... Alex is very cautious about who she lets into her life.'

Callum smiled. 'Yes, I've begun to realise that over this last couple of months. It hasn't been easy, getting to know her as well as I'd like.'

'Well, just as long as you do right by her. I love my sister. I don't want to see her hurt.'

'I'll take good care of her, you have my word,' Callum said.

Alex sent him an uncertain look. That sounded as though he meant it. Did it mean he was planning on staying around, being part of her life?

They left her brother a few minutes later so that he could get some rest. 'Sarah will be so happy when she hears the news,' Alex said as they walked out to the car park.

Callum nodded, laying a reassuring palm on the small of her back. 'You must be relieved. Perhaps now that your mind's at ease you'll be able to relax and enjoy the rest of the afternoon.'

'Definitely,' she said, looking up at him and drinking in his features. For the first time in ages she felt as though life held some very real promise.

Suddenly, the quiet was disturbed by the bleeping of Callum's phone. His mouth flattened. 'Sorry about this,' he said, gently releasing her so that he could answer the call.

He spoke to the person on the other end of the line for a minute or two. 'Thanks, Katie,' he said after a while, and Alex looked at him curiously. Why would Katie be phoning him?

'It's good news,' he said, cutting the call and

putting his phone back into his pocket. 'The board has posted its decision—the A and E unit is safe. They're going to follow some of your suggestions to bring in money from outside. And it looks as though my mini-stroke unit is a go, as well.' He grinned. 'You realise, don't you, Miss Bean Counter, this means I'll probably get my Doppler ultrasound machine after all?'

'Oh, Callum, that's great news.' She flung her arms around him. 'I hardly dared hope they'd go for it.' Then she leaned back a fraction and looked him in the eyes. 'Bean Counter?' she said, lifting a brow. 'Is that going to be my title for evermore?'

'Hmm. I'll have to think about that. Maybe we could change it for something else.'

'I should hope so.'

He smiled. 'Perhaps we should be on our way. I'm starving, so I think we should find a place to eat first of all.' He pulled open the car door for her. 'I know this great place just as you come into Cheddar.'

'Another one? How come I don't know these places?'

'Probably because you've had your nose to the grindstone for way too long. It's high time you learned how to loosen up and enjoy life.'

'And you'll show me how to do that?'

'Oh, yes.' His blue gaze travelled over her, his eyes filled with promise. 'I'm making it my very next project.'

He set the car in motion, and headed for the main road that would take them towards the Mendip Hills and on to Cheddar. Alex watched as the landscape changed from gentle slopes to rugged hills and deep gorges. It felt strangely as though she was travelling towards some new destiny, but perhaps that was due to the sheer excitement of being with him on this glorious afternoon, free as a bird for once. She wasn't going to think about the future, she decided. She was just going to take life as it came.

They stopped at a pretty, stone-built inn, made colourful with window-boxes full of flowers and hanging baskets spilling over with bright surfinias and trailing silver-leaved ivy.

'We could sit outside, if you like,' Callum said, leading the way through the inn and showing her the gardens through the open glass doors. There were bench tables set out in a courtyard that had been decorated with foliage plants and tubs of scarlet begonias. Beyond that were landscaped gardens, where flowering shrubs bordered a wide sweep of lawn.

'Yes, please, that would be lovely.' She could feel the sun warm on her bare arms, and on her legs where her light cotton skirt flowed delicately and skimmed her calves.

For his meal, Callum chose fillets of sea bass, served on a bed of roasted vegetables, whilst Alex went for a pork steak, topped with an apple-and-cider relish, and finished off under the grill with Cheddar cheese.

'They make the cheese just along the road from here,' Callum murmured, as he watched her spear the topping with her fork. 'Have you heard the legend about how it came to be made?'

'No, I haven't.'

'Well, apparently a milkmaid left a pail of milk in one of the Cheddar caves, and returned some time later to find that it had turned into a tasty cheese. Whether that's true or not, I don't know, but even today they mature the cheeses in Gough's Cave, wrapped in muslin cheesecloth. They say the tangy taste is due to the rich grazing pastures around here.'

'So if we visit Gough's Cave, we'll see them?' She thought about that. 'And probably smell them.'

He chuckled and lifted his fork to taste the succulent fish. 'Among other things, yes.'

Some time later, full up and satisfied after a meal that had been finished off with fresh fruit salad and liqueur coffees, they set off in the car once again. Alex was relaxed and happy. Her only niggling desire was that Callum should put his arms around her, but of course he wouldn't do that. They were in a public place…and she couldn't help wishing that they could be somewhere else where they could be totally, utterly alone.

He sent her an oblique glance as they drove along the road towards Cheddar. 'You're very quiet. Is everything okay? You're not worried about your brother, are you?'

'No, I'm fine. I'm sure he's going to be okay.

I'm having a great time. It's just good to be out here under a perfect blue sky, and it's taking me a while to get used to it.' It wasn't like her to be this way…hung up on getting close to a man…but Callum was different. He was gentle and thoughtful, and it was totally restful, being with him.

They were opposites, though. He was good for her, but was she good for him? She'd always been ambitious, following her career, and by all accounts that was the kind of woman he would rather steer clear of in the long term.

It was some half an hour later when they reached Cheddar Gorge. The scenery was spectacular, and Alex marvelled at the ravine, and its sheer-sided cliffs, cut out of ancient limestone. The banks were rich with greenery, and there was the occasional crop of wildflowers here and there, adding tiny patches of colour.

'Have you been here before?' Callum asked as he parked the car.

She shook her head. 'I've heard all about it, though. They say it was formed by a river some three million years ago, and then the Ice Age came, and after that the meltwater carved out the gorge.'

'I think that's probably right. Shall we go and take a look at Gough's Cave? It's the biggest one, and it's well worth seeing.'

'It would be a shame not to, while we're here.'

'Good.' He clasped her hand in his and she felt the thrill of his touch glide along her arm like a ripple of warm silk. They walked to the cave and went inside, and before long Alex was marvelling at the weird and wonderful formations that had been brought about by water dripping through the limestone over millions of years.

It was awe-inspiring. In one chamber, impressive stalactites were reflected in a pool below, giving an impression of a village perched on a mountain top. In another chamber, huge stalagmites reached high up into the roof and water droplets were reflected in the cavern's lights so that they sparkled like crystal.

Alex shivered slightly in the cool atmosphere, and Callum immediately took off his light jacket and wrapped it around her, drawing her close. 'We can't have you getting cold,' he said. 'We don't want you ending up like the man they found in here, do we?'

Alex was shocked. 'What man? What happened to him?'

Callum laughed softly. 'He was young, apparently, and he was buried here some nine thousand years ago. His skeleton was found intact, and they've even managed to extract DNA from his tooth cavity, to show that he still has relatives living in the area.'

'You're joking!'

'No, it's true, believe me.'

She smiled. 'That's some family history—if you were searching for your ancestors, you'd hardly expect to go so far back, would you?'

'You wouldn't.' He held her close, walking with her back through the caves, until they emerged out into the sunlight once more.

She handed him his jacket. 'Thanks for that,' she said. She was reluctant to let it go. It had been warm from his body, and it had bought her nearer to him than she had been for what seemed like a long time.

He slung it over his shoulder, holding it with

one hand, while he clasped her fingers with the other. 'Shall we walk by the river for a while?' he suggested.

'Yes, that sounds good.' She looked up at him. 'Somehow, I don't want the day to end. I know it must, eventually, but it's been so good, I want it to go on and on.'

He laid his arm around her shoulders. 'That's how I feel, too, and I think it's done you a world of good. You needed a break after all that's been happening. You certainly look better for it. There's colour in your cheeks and your eyes are sparkling.'

They walked towards the fields and the river, taking their time, ambling along and enjoying the lushness of nature all around them. By the riverside, Alex spotted a kingfisher searching for prey in the water, and further on there were two white egrets, shuffling their feet in the shallows.

It was glorious and so peaceful, and they stopped and sat for a while on the grassy bank in the shade of a broad oak tree, watching the sunlight playing over the water.

Callum eased himself closer to her. He looked

at her, his gaze wandering over her features, over the smooth line of her cheekbones and the soft curve of her cheek. Then he bent his head and dropped a kiss on to her soft mouth, surprising her and starting up an array of tingling sensations that ran from her lips right down to the soft centre of her abdomen.

'Oh,' she said huskily. 'What was that for?'

'Just because.'

'Because what?'

'Because it was something I just had to do. Because your lips are soft and inviting and it's all I can do to resist you.' His fingers caressed her cheek. 'Because I've been wanting to do that all day.'

'Oh.' She was finally speechless. She gazed up at him, loving the feeling of being close to him, of having his long body mesh with hers.

His blue eyes glinted, his gaze trailing over her as though he would absorb her features into his memory.

'It's been great to see you looking so relaxed. We'll have to find more opportunities to take time out and explore different places together. I want to spend a lot more time with you.'

'Funny, that...I was thinking the same thing.'

He nodded. 'It doesn't matter where...the beach, meadow walks, your place or mine...just as long as we're together.'

She smiled at him. 'It's what I want, too.' She was quiet for a moment. 'Strange, isn't it, that I've never seen your place? I was beginning to wonder if it was some kind of sacred bachelor pad...your very own sanctuary.' Her expression became wistful. 'You more or less said that's what you intended when you bought it.'

His mouth made a crooked shape. 'People change. I changed...at least, I changed when I met you.' His glance flicked over her. 'I'm not alone in that, am I? Hasn't the same thing happened to you? You used to live in a rented place, and then you came down here and bought that rambling old property. I always wondered why you took it on, especially at a time when you had so much else on your plate. I think your subconscious mind was telling you that you needed to settle down, to be part of a family unit, and that house would be the one place where you sensed could be truly happy.'

'You think so?'

'Mmm-hmm. Though it's going to be a little more crowded than you expected, quite soon, from the sound of things, when your brother and his wife move in with you. I think it's great that you're doing it, but are you going to be happy with that?' He tugged her closer to him as though he needed to feel the softness of her curves against his taut, masculine body. His hands stroked the small of her back, moving over the swell of her hips.

'I think so.' She snuggled up against him, cherishing the moment. 'I want to see Ross and his family reunited, and they need somewhere to stay while they recover from their injuries. Beth's come on by leaps and bounds, and I'm sure she'll soon regain her strength. I think Ross will take a little longer, and he needs to be perfectly fit before they can go house-hunting...unless Beth does it for them. At least his job is being kept open for him. The company wants him back.'

Callum smiled. 'That's good.' He lowered his

head to hers and kissed her once again, taking his time, exploring the softness of her lips, moving against her as though he couldn't get enough of her.

Alex was in seventh heaven. This was way more than she could have hoped for, to have him kiss her and hold her and make her feel that she was everything to him just then. She ran her hands over his shoulders, his arms, trailing her fingers over the length of his spine.

'That feels so good,' he murmured, his voice roughened as he dragged his mouth reluctantly from hers. 'But every time I hold you I think it's not nearly enough. I want us to be together.'

She gave him a cautious look from under her lashes. 'I'm not sure what you're asking.'

He laid his cheek against hers. 'Do you think you might want to move in with me for a while, once Ross and Beth are settled in your house? I know my apartment is a bit small, after what you're used to, but we can at least be together, alone, private.'

She hesitated, drawing back a little and laying her palms flatly against his chest as she looked up at him. 'You're suggesting we live together?' Was he saying he wanted just a casual fling, no strings attached? Her spirits plummeted. She wanted so much more than that.

He nodded. 'Just until Ross and Beth find a place of their own. I mean, I really like the children, and it's great having them around, and I'm sure I'll get along fine with your brother and his wife...but I really would like to have you to myself for a while. I know it's a lot to ask of you, but once they find their own house, I can put my apartment on the market.'

She frowned. 'Why would you want to do that?'

'Like I said, I've changed. Why would I need a bachelor apartment any longer? I've fallen in love with a woman who has the perfect family home. We could spend a lifetime together there.'

Her mouth dropped open a little. 'Is this your way of telling me that you love me?'

He nodded. 'I do love you, Alex. We're like two opposite halves, but we fit together so well. I just know we could make it work...if you would agree to be my wife. After all, you said you didn't want to be Miss Bean Counter, didn't you? Mrs Brooksby has a nice ring to it, don't you think?'

A soft sigh escaped her. 'I thought you were asking me to move in with you, for us to live together without any kind of commitment.' She looked up at him, her expression quizzical. 'I thought you said you never felt the need to settle down, that marriage and commitment weren't for you?'

He nodded. 'That was all true...until I met you. Then after that everything was different. It took me a while to realise what was happening. I couldn't believe that I'd fallen for someone who was so strong and career minded—the very opposite of what I thought I wanted—but you showed me that you know instinctively what's more important. You showed it when you came down to Somerset to look after Sarah and James, and you showed it again when you took the time off work to be with them. I know things are going to work out just fine for us, Alex.' He looked at her intently. 'I just need you to tell me that you love me too, and that you want me as much as I want you.'

'I do.' She gave a soft sigh. 'I never knew that I could feel this way. I never met anyone who could make me feel the way you do. You're so calm and relaxed, you don't let things throw you, and you know exactly how to cajole me into seeing what really matters. And at the same time you're single-minded and so good at what you do. You're the perfect man for me...the only man for me.'

She tilted her face to his and kissed him tenderly. 'I love you,' she murmured. 'More than anything in the world. And I'd love to be your wife and move into your apartment...' her mouth curved '...just as long as we get back to the farmhouse as soon as possible.'

He breathed a sigh of relief. 'That's just wonderful. For a long while, I've felt as though there was something missing from my life, but now I feel complete. Just as long as I have you, life will be everything I ever wanted.'

'Funny, isn't it?' she said softly, reaching up to kiss him once more. 'That's exactly how I feel.'

* * * * *

Mills & Boon® Large Print
Medical

December

FLIRTING WITH THE SOCIETY DOCTOR   Janice Lynn
WHEN ONE NIGHT ISN'T ENOUGH   Wendy S. Marcus
MELTING THE ARGENTINE DOCTOR'S HEART   Meredith Webber
SMALL TOWN MARRIAGE MIRACLE   Jennifer Taylor
ST PIRAN'S: PRINCE ON THE CHILDREN'S WARD   Sarah Morgan
HARRY ST CLAIR: ROGUE OR DOCTOR?   Fiona McArthur

January

THE PLAYBOY OF HARLEY STREET   Anne Fraser
DOCTOR ON THE RED CARPET   Anne Fraser
JUST ONE LAST NIGHT…   Amy Andrews
SUDDENLY SINGLE SOPHIE   Leonie Knight
THE DOCTOR & THE RUNAWAY HEIRESS   Marion Lennox
THE SURGEON SHE NEVER FORGOT   Melanie Milburne

February

CAREER GIRL IN THE COUNTRY   Fiona Lowe
THE DOCTOR'S REASON TO STAY   Dianne Drake
WEDDING ON THE BABY WARD   Lucy Clark
SPECIAL CARE BABY MIRACLE   Lucy Clark
THE TORTURED REBEL   Alison Roberts
DATING DR DELICIOUS   Laura Iding